THE HAVEN

NICOLA MARSH

For the readers who loved The Retreat so much, your feedback meant I had to write a sequel. I had no choice but to give those dastardly characters another outing...

You can run, but you can't hide...

The Haven, a refuge for many, is Rylee's home, and her grandmother Leah is her hero. Rylee wants to continue her gran's good work with those less fortunate, but is keen to expand her horizons after leading a sheltered life. When an opportunity to work at Arcania, a wellness retreat, lands in Rylee's lap, she's rapt.

But her grandmother disapproves, and as Rylee embarks on a quest to discover her biological family, secrets from the past unravel at terrifying speed.

Decades earlier, Leah flees a tragedy and arrives at The Haven. The creepy house provides the sanctuary she craves. When she gets a job at nearby Arcania, she's intrigued by the gothic mansion and its inhabitants, but witnesses horrors that send her running.

Now, her precious granddaughter shares her fascination for Arcania, putting Rylee in harm's way.

How far will Leah go to protect the ones she loves?

PROLOGUE

Fear is a terrible thing.

It's insidious, worming its way into every aspect of your life until you're on edge all the time.

I can't label the fear that dogs me every day.

Fear of the unknown?

Fear of exposure?

Fear I'll lose everyone that matters to me because of what I've done?

So I fake it.

I pretend like nothing is wrong. I spread joy. I lavish love. I'm a do-gooder.

But what happens when the good you do is penance for the bad?

Do a few altruistic deeds cancel out the horror?

I'm not sure, but for now, my quest to be a better person has to be enough. Because the past is catching up with me. I can feel it, one step behind me, its fetid breath brushing the back of my neck.

I can't outrun it.

So I have two choices.
Make a stand and fight.
Or die trying.

RYLEE

NOW

D o you ever get a bad feeling? A sense of impending doom that no matter what you do, your life is about to go awry?

I've had that feeling for a while now, ever since I finished high school a few months ago. Maybe it's just fear of the future because I don't know what I want to do with my life? Maybe it's more an inkling that something isn't right in my perfect family?

I have an idea where it stems from. Ever since I had to do an assignment in biology on genes, I've been wondering about where I came from. My dad and gran raised me, and I've lived in Edgewater Bay my entire life, but I've been homeschooled and sheltered for the last eighteen years. I want to know about my mom and her side of the family, but the few times I've asked Gran over the years she clams up, and questioning Dad is useless because he can't remember.

He has dissociative amnesia and has no memories of his life before he walked into The Haven twenty years ago. That's where we live, The Haven, a mansion on the outskirts of Edgewater Bay. We're isolated, with our nearest neighbor over two miles away, and growing up, I loved the house's spooky vibe. I also loved how we had a never-ending stream of new people living here. Gran is rich and from the time she arrived here almost forty years ago, she's let those who need a place to stay live here.

She's my hero and a small part of me wants to help her run The Haven and continue her good work. But a larger part of me wants to spread my wings and see what the world has to offer. To explore my background.

To find my mom.

"Hey." Dad snaps his fingers in front of my face. "That dill won't chop itself."

I poke my tongue out at him. "Cooking with you is supposed to be relaxing, but all you do is order me around."

The corners of his eyes crinkle when he smiles. "It's the only time I get to boss anyone around."

We laugh because we know that Gran's in charge around here. Leah Smith is a formidable force who's respected in town, and because she keeps to herself, she's somewhat of a legend too. The few times we go into Edgewater Bay, I sense people staring at us. It's not overt, it's more of an intangible feeling.

When I was younger, I'd cling to Gran's hand because being out of the house scared me. The Haven made me feel safe. Ironic, considering now that I'm eighteen, I can't wait to escape its confines.

"You okay, Lee?"

Dad's the only one who abbreviates my name, and I like it. We're close and I've wished many times over the years that I could help him remember what his life was like before coming here. I see his confusion sometimes, a glazed look in his eyes like he's struggling with something.

I researched dissociative amnesia years ago, and it involves a breakdown of memory, awareness, and identity, usually after enduring or witnessing a traumatic event, like an accident, disaster, or abuse. I hate the thought of my gentle dad being subjected to any of that and I think it's why I haven't pushed him for answers. Who knows what jogging his memory might uncover?

Because that's the thing with dissociative amnesia; the person still has memories but they're buried so deep they can't be recalled. And that means they must be bad. But I also read that the memories might resurface on their own, or be triggered by something in a person's surroundings, and a small part of me hopes this might happen one day.

"Hey." He touches my arm, concern creasing his brow. "What's going on? You're totally spaced out."

I force a smile, wishing I could badger him for answers to the many questions buzzing in my head.

What happened to you?

Why don't you want to remember?

What will you do if I leave?

Ultimately, that's what's keeping me here. It's not fair that caring for my dad falls on Gran. She has enough to do with running The Haven. Besides, I'm the only biological family my dad has as far as we know, and that means I need to step up.

"I'm fine, Dad. Just thinking about the future."

"It's not too late to apply to colleges, you know."

"I know." Though spending years studying and sharing

a dorm isn't my idea of spreading my wings. If I leave home, I want to have adventures, not be stuck in one place. "But I really want to take a gap year and figure out stuff."

Namely, find my mom.

I haven't mentioned it to Gran because I know she'll freak, which is annoying considering she'd be the best person to ask. Dad has never mentioned my mother, so I've avoided asking him. I'm always tiptoeing around him, scared of what prompting him to remember might unravel.

But I need to start somewhere. Besides, Mom couldn't have been part of his memory loss because he met her after he arrived here.

"What does figuring out stuff mean?" He asks, giving me the perfect opening to probe him for information about my mother.

I lead into it gently. "Working out what I want to do with my life. Places I want to visit." I inhale softly, steeling my nerve. "Finding out more about Mom."

The knife he's holding clatters to the countertop, and I hate the flash of pain across his face that I've caused.

"You've told me nothing about her all these years," I rush on, "and it's only natural I'm curious. So I hope we can talk about her now?"

His sigh is resigned, and he pinches the bridge of his nose before lowering his hand and fixing me with a solemn stare. "I guess I should apologize for not discussing her with you, but I won't because I'm not sorry." He shrugs. "I wanted to protect you from the pain I endured when your mother abandoned us."

"So she just up and left one day?"

He nods, a lingering hurt darkening his eyes. "Robyn arrived here eight months after I did. She said she had no family either and we were drawn to each other." His smile is soft. "The morning she gave birth to you was the happiest day of my life. She chose the name Rylee, after a heroine in a book she loved. Then, ten days later, she left to go pick up formula and diapers, and didn't come back…"

He trails off, his gaze fixed on some point over my shoulder. "Your Gran stepped up. I took the night feeds because I couldn't sleep, I was that distraught, but she helped with everything else. We wanted to lavish you with love to make up for Robyn leaving…"

He shakes his head. "I'll never understand how she could've done it. You were the most precious baby, an unexpected gift neither of us expected, but were determined to love nonetheless. Raising you was all she talked about in the months leading up to the birth. We wanted to get a place together, a small cottage somewhere where we could be a family. So when she left and didn't return, it was unfathomable."

My chest aches and my eyes burn with the effort of holding back tears. Dad sounds so forlorn, but I'm glad I asked him about Mom. Not that what he's divulged has helped. If anything, I now have more questions.

What would drive away a young mom who seemed smitten with the idea of raising her baby and building a life as a family?

"And you never tried to find her?"

"I had you to look after, and your grandmother discouraged it."

"Why wouldn't Gran want to find her?"

A deep groove dents his forehead. "Your gran's always been protective of me. And I trust her implicitly, which is why I agreed at the time that no good could come of forcing Robyn to return here even if we found her. Plus, I was angry at her, furious that she could abandon you and the life we'd planned."

I hate how broken Dad sounds, and I wrap my arms around him. "Sorry for bringing up bad memories."

"It's okay, honey." He rests his cheek on top of my head and hugs me tight. "You're old enough to know the truth now."

But that's the thing. What is the truth? And why did my grandmother, with all her resources and money, not want to find my mother?

Only one way to find out.

Time to have a chat with Gran.

CHAPTER

TWO

LEAH

THEN

I can pinpoint the exact moment the loathing for my parents turned to hatred.

Precisely three minutes ago, when the doctor delivered the devastating news that my baby had died and I wouldn't be able to have more children.

I watch his lips move, the callous words about 'complications' and 'infertility' delivered in a neutral tone he probably uses all day every day, before he leaves the room and a nurse enters.

I'm numb from more than the aftereffects of anesthetic. I can't feel a thing inside, apart from that flicker of hate for Don and Judy Smith, society darlings of Harrisburg, who'd forced me into this. The flicker grows into an inferno as the enormity of what they've done swamps me anew and I know that the second I'm discharged, I'm leaving North Carolina without looking back.

Ironic that they'd seen this pregnancy as a mere blip in their plan for my life and once 'taken care of' I'd head off to college without a second thought.

As if.

That's the thing about having rich, narcissistic parents. They'd actually set up a special bank account for me moving forward when I know what it is.

Hush money.

The moment I'd mentioned keeping the baby, they'd tried to buy me off. Not that I'd decided either way at the time, but they couldn't tolerate a scandal and the thought of their eighteen-year-old daughter being unwed and having a baby had sent them into damage control. Meaning I have ten million dollars in my account for 'college expenses.'

Good luck with that plan, Mom and Dad.

The nurse hovers by my bedside, making an ineffectual show of checking my blood pressure and heart rate while darting concerned glances at me like she expects I'll leap out of bed at any moment and make a run for it.

"How are you feeling?" She asks, her smile genuine despite her inane question.

I want to yell, 'how the hell do you think I'm feeling when I've just given birth to a dead baby and my heart is fractured?' but none of this is her fault. She's doing her job.

"I've been better." My voice is croaky, and my throat hurts when I try to clear it.

"Press the buzzer if you need anything," she says, with a sympathetic pat on my arm. Like she has any idea how I'm feeling.

My anger is swelling, filling me with a burning need to get out of here. But I'm too weak. And I have some unfinished business.

Ensuring my parents know they lost me the moment I lost my child.

"Are my folks outside?"

She nods. "Shall I send them in?"

"Yes, please."

I can't fathom why she tenses, until I realize she must've already met Don and Judy and been subjected to their special brand of 'we're entitled, and you better do as we say or else'.

"Don't forget you can buzz me any time," she says, as if reinforcing she'll help me confront my folks if I need her.

Her thoughtfulness brings tears to my eyes, and I bite my bottom lip to stop from bawling. Mom and Dad equate crying with weakness, something I learned at four, when I'd burst into tears after being forced to eat a mouthful of caviar because they expected me to be their perfect party accessory. Smacking kids may not be condoned by many, but Don and Judy didn't subscribe to the nurturing parenting philosophy. I swear my butt had hurt for a week.

"Thanks," I murmur, and she casts me a final concerned glance before opening the door.

My folks barely wait for the nurse to leave before they barge into the room, wearing matching expressions of indignation. Nobody keeps the Smiths waiting.

"You look fine," Dad says, his bushy brows drawing together in a frown as he barely glances at the beeping medical paraphernalia I'm hooked up to that shows I'm alive.

"Yes, very good," Mom adds, her mouth pursed in distaste at the sight of me in a pale blue hospital gown rather than the designer gear she'd prefer me in.

I hadn't expected pleasantries, but a simple 'how are you?' or 'we're sorry' would've been preferable to their fake gusto. It proves what I already know. They don't care about me. I'm an accessory, like the priceless painting hanging in the den. Something to parade around to their equally phony friends.

It's why we flew to Palm Springs months ago, before I was showing, and they paid an exorbitant sum to a lawyer to facilitate a private adoption. And why they checked me in to this expensive hospital that caters to the rich and famous for the birth. Discretion guaranteed. And far from Harrisburg, where anyone might hear rumors of Leah Smith being knocked up after graduating high school.

They would've told their friends we were taking a family trip to celebrate my graduation. Only the three of us know the truth. Not even Chad Lipinski—the guy voted most likely to end up in prison in our yearbook—who I'd deliberately given my virginity to because he's the exact opposite of every guy my parents have tried to set me up with, doesn't know. I may have slept with him out of spite for my rigid family values, but I have no intention of being shackled to him as co-parents.

I had a different plan when I discovered I was pregnant. Move to the Outer Banks, my favorite place in the world, and raise my baby alone, far from the reach of my parents.

But when my defiance made me blurt the truth over a fraught family dinner, they'd threatened to cut me off and I'd been terrified of raising a child on my own with no financial support. I know many have done it and I admire those women, but I'm not that strong. They browbeat me with so many horrific scenarios that in the end I'd agreed to give my baby up for adoption to shut them up.

I never expected to feel this...bereft. Grieving for a baby I didn't know I truly wanted until it was too late.

I hate them. For this and for everything that has come before.

I'm done.

"Are you still sedated?" My father peers at me through narrowed eyes, like he can't fathom why I'm not responding to their inane observation about how 'good' I look. "Say something."

I bite back every curse I'd like to fling in their faces and settle for, "Is your annual fundraiser going ahead next week?"

It's a stupid question, but one I've asked to lead into my threat. Don and Judy are on the board of many Harrisburg charities and the one for mental health issues in young people is by far the biggest. They preside over a lavish ball annually and raise millions of dollars courtesy of their cronies who don't like to be upstaged. The event is a sellout. I'm counting on it. Five hundred of Mom and Dad's closest allies who will hear the truth if my folks don't do as I say.

"Of course the ball is next week, darling." Mom's fingertips graze the back of my hand in a fleeting gesture that's her version of affection. "Your dress is ready to be picked up from the designer—"

"I won't be there," I say, surprised my voice doesn't quiver. "I'm leaving Harrisburg and you're going to give me full access to my trust fund, with that additional ten million dollars you gave me to shut me up."

My father barks out a laugh. "Whatever drugs they've given you have made you crazy. We'll talk about this when you're discharged."

Mom's not laughing. She's staring at me, confused but wary. We may not be close, but she's more observant than Dad and the obstinate press of my lips must alert her I'm not kidding.

"If you want to go on a vacation, Leah, we'll certainly fund that. A pleasant break in a luxury hotel might be just what you need—"

"I don't want a vacation, Mom. I'm leaving. And I'm not coming back. Ever."

Mom's mouth drops open and Dad's face flushes puce.

"I won't hear any more of this nonsense." His bellow is so loud Mom flinches. "We'll discuss you taking a vacation after we get home."

He makes a grand show of looking at the gold watch that costs more than what a nurse would earn in a year. "Come on, Judy. She needs to rest."

Mom takes a hesitant step toward Dad, as if she's reluctant to leave me but will never disobey him. She never does.

I want to end this once and for all, so I deliver the threat I know will get me exactly what I want.

Freedom.

"If you don't give me the money and access to my trust fund, I'll announce to the world that you forced me to give my baby up for adoption, but it died anyway."

This time, Dad joins Mom in open-mouthed shock, and I press the buzzer to summon the nurse to stave off the inevitable tantrum he'll throw. Thankfully, she must've been nearby and appears as Dad takes a step toward the bed, his rage evident in the muscles of his neck standing out like cords.

The nurse takes one look at my face and says, "Visiting hours are over. Leah needs to rest."

I could've hugged her, managing a grateful smile instead.

Dad leans down on the pretext of pressing a kiss to my forehead, but I hear his muttered, "You disgust me. We'll talk about this madness later."

"Love you too, Dad," I say, loud enough that Mom shoots me a suspicious glance.

But she says nothing. She pats my leg and follows my father as he storms out, leaving me hollow but victorious.

I know I've won.

THREE

RYLEE

NOW

I find Gran in the backyard, surveying the vegetable garden. It's her pet project, something she started many years ago, so those who pass through The Haven could have a practical task to do. The huge patch always needed tending—mulching, weeding, pruning, picking—and it never fails to soothe, what with the distant sound of the ocean a peaceful backdrop.

I had my own tiny shovel, hoe and pitchfork set when I was little and I loved kneeling in the dirt alongside her, poking at clumps, planting seeds, picking strawberries. It's our thing and I'm glad she's out here now, as it might make her more amenable to what I have to ask.

She has her back to me, my footsteps swallowed by the grass as I approach, but she somehow hears me.

"Just in time, Rylee, I'm about to start weeding."

I grimace and wrap my arms around her from behind. "Will a hug get me out of it?"

"Unlikely." She chuckles and I release her, forever grateful that this woman has been the one constant in my life, even if my mother hasn't.

She turns to face me, her serene expression a direct result of spending time in this garden. It's the only time I see her this relaxed because my gran's one of those people who can never sit still. I often wonder if that's why she opened her house to others, because she likes to be kept busy and caring for those in need gives her a purpose.

A part of me wants to continue her legacy, to stay here and help her, but a larger part of me craves freedom. A chance to see what exists beyond this house, this town. Gran and Dad mean everything to me, but it's time. I've never had a boyfriend. Heck, I've never been kissed, and the only friends I have are Gran's friends, Mel and Freda, which is kind of pathetic.

Gran's overprotective and doesn't let me get too close to the people who pass through The Haven, especially teens my age. I'd liked a boy once, Drake, a nineteen-year-old musician who arrived about six months ago with a guitar strapped to his back and his blond hair tied in a man bun with a frayed leather band. He had the dreamiest eyes, aquamarine bordering on green, and I'd been smitten. I'd tried to hide it from Gran, but she'd noticed—probably didn't help that I blushed whenever he entered a room— and sadly, he'd vanished on his third day here.

I'd aimed for casual when asking Gran about him, but she'd seen right through me and proceeded to lecture me on the importance of finishing high school and not being distracted by drifters.

"You're daydreaming," she says, her matter-of-fact tone underlined by curiosity. "What's gotten into you?"

Gran's always said I'm pragmatic, like her, so the fact I've drifted off in her presence is cause for her slight frown.

"I want to ask you about Mom," I say, not surprised when her expression instantly blanks. She's an expert at hiding emotion. "And I don't want you avoiding my questions."

There's a flicker of unease in her eyes before she responds. "I'm surprised it's taken you this long to ask."

"It's because any time I've hinted at wanting to know more, you've shut down and I like confrontation about as much as you do."

Her smile is sheepish. "I hate discussing anything remotely uncomfortable, and I didn't want to cause you pain by talking about your mother."

"I'm a big girl now, Gran. So give it to me straight. Do you know why she left?"

She hesitates before pointing to a nearby bench. "Let's sit."

A splinter of wood pierces the back of my thigh as I take a seat beside her, but the pain doesn't register. I'm too enthralled by the look in my grandmother's eyes—part fear, part regret.

"When Robyn Leetham arrived here, she told me she had no family, but she had an expensive duffel filled with decent clothes, a stylish haircut, and beautiful skin that suggested she hadn't been doing it tough like many of the others who drift in and out of The Haven. But as you know, I never push for information. We offer sanctuary without pressure, but I had an inkling Robyn would be trouble."

"Why?"

"She had a sly edge, so you can imagine my chagrin

when your father fell for her almost instantly." Her frown deepens. "He'd been here for just over a year when Robyn arrived, and I'd never seen him so happy." She sighs. "It made me happy too, because I hated seeing him so disjointed, unable to remember anything about his life before arriving here. But their lighthearted flirtation quickly turned serious when Robyn discovered she was pregnant."

"How did she feel about that?"

Gran shrugs. "Happy enough, I guess, but she never really opened up to me, and I could never fully trust that what she was telling your father was the truth, so who really knows? For your father's sake, I offered all the support I could. Setting up a nursery. Organizing a home birth as she wanted. Doing whatever I could to make life easy for them, because I could see that despite their bravado they were terrified of becoming parents."

"Sounds like you were supportive."

Gran nods. "As her due date grew closer, I could see Robyn withdraw."

"What do you mean?"

"She didn't smile much. She didn't talk to me at all and only responded to your father with fleeting answers. She spent all day in her room. She hardly ate. Then she went into labor..." Gran reaches out and grasps my hand. I'm glad for her warmth, as my hand is icy. "It all happened so fast, nothing like the books we'd read, so the midwife didn't make it and I delivered you."

My mouth drops open. "How did I not know that?"

Her smile is bashful. "Because that would mean discussing your mother, and I didn't want to do that."

"What happened next?"

"I would've said Robyn had postpartum depression, but

she'd already withdrawn before the birth, so it was more of the same." She squeezes my hand. "It broke my heart to see her want nothing to do with you. She didn't want to feed you or change you or hold you. Your father and I made sure you were cared for. I tried talking to her and suggested she see a doctor, but she freaked out and I left her alone. I thought time would heal whatever ailed her, that she'd grow to love you the more time she spent with you, but ten days after she gave birth to you, she left."

"And you never went after her? Searched for her? Tried to convince her to come back?"

Gran's lips compress, and she blinks rapidly. "I'm ashamed to say a small part of me was relieved when she left. You were the most adorable baby and I couldn't comprehend how Robyn couldn't love you as much as we did. I'd never taken to her and it made me dislike her even more. Besides, she'd broken your father's heart and I could never forgive her for that."

Way to go with holding a grudge, Gran.

I'm baffled, because while a realist, my grandmother is also the most compassionate person I know. She'd have to be, to take in so many homeless and give them shelter, food, and clothing, asking nothing in return. So for her to not search for my mother, especially if she had suspicions of depression, seems heartless.

"And you've never heard from her since? She's never tried to contact you?"

Astute as always, Gran knows what I'm really asking: Did my mother ever reach out to me?

She slips an arm around my shoulders. "I'm sorry, Rylee, she never contacted us again."

A swift pain slashes my chest and I lean into my gran as her arm around my shoulders tightens.

I can't fathom that my mother abandoned me and never wanted to know me. Maybe her mental health issues were more severe than Gran thought, and she mightn't have survived? The thought saddens me.

I should be thankful Gran has opened up, but I feel emptier than before. And not that I'll tell her, but I know only one thing will settle the persistent niggle deep down.

Discovering what happened to my mother after she left The Haven.

CHAPTER

FOUR

LEAH

THEN

The day after my 'procedure', as my parents call it, they agree to my terms: full access to my trust fund and the extra ten million dollars in my account.

The next day, I'm back home in Harrisburg, packing my things, and I find a house online that I buy sight-unseen. The realtor is stunned. I'm ecstatic.

Four days later, my parents are dressed in their finest for the charity ball, ignoring me as I wait beside my car to say goodbye.

I wish this could've been different, that we could've been the kind of family who supports and loves each other unconditionally. But we're not and never have been, so there's no point hoping they'll change at this late stage.

"Bye Mom. Bye Dad," I call out, knowing it's futile. I'm dead to them. Dad said as much when I tried to explain why I'm doing this. Mom remained stoic, but her disapproval was palpable.

They don't understand that they made me this way. They caused this. All I've ever wanted is to be part of a family that's close and understanding and inclusive of more than fast cars and a twelve-room mansion.

I know that's why I wanted to keep my baby. Deep down, a part of me wanted to create my own family if the one I'd been born into was such a disappointment. But my baby is dead and I'm grieving. My parents don't care. I would've been sad if I'd given the baby up for adoption as planned, but I would've known he or she was alive, and that would've been a small consolation. But knowing the baby I'd carried for nine months had been stillborn...it breaks my heart.

The lump of sadness in my throat swells as I watch my parents get into the town car without a backward glance. The chauffeur shoots me a puzzled glance as he opens the driver's door. He's picked us up on many occasions and I always accompany my folks. I almost raise my hand in a half-hearted wave before realizing how stupid that'll look; farewelling a driver when my own parents have eschewed any kind of goodbye.

As the car glides away, the tears I've been battling finally fall. I press the back of my hand to my mouth to stop the sobs as I watch the car's taillights all the way to the curve in the road until they disappear. It's stupid, because a small part of me still hoped they'd change their minds, that they'd apologize for being cold and callous and beg me to stay.

I should've known better.

My chest is aching—from subduing sobs or for losing my family, I'm not sure—but I can't stand around here wishing for things that'll never happen. It'll take me eight hours to get to the Outer Banks if I don't stop. I know it's not smart to drive through the night and arrive in a new place in the wee hours of the morning, but I can't stand to spend another minute here. Besides, the realtor already couriered a set of keys to me, so it won't matter if I arrive at three in the morning.

Despite the urge, I don't glance over my shoulder at the French Provincial mansion that has been my home for the last eighteen years. Instead, I get in my car, start the engine, and leave the circular drive without looking back.

I ARRIVE in Edgewater Bay at three-thirty-three a.m. I take it as a good omen. I can do with a change of luck. I'd only stopped once for gas and coffee. Not that I needed the caffeine to stay alert. I'm buzzed at the prospect of living on my own for the first time and having a fresh start, far from the frosty silences and frigid glares of my judgmental parents, who I'm determined not to miss despite the loneliness clawing at my heart.

I'd asked the realtor to leave the lights on in my house but as I crest Oceanview Drive and get my first glimpse of the ten room, five bathroom 'shack' I purchased, it's in darkness.

Silhouetted against a cloudless inky sky, it's both welcoming and intimidating at the same time. Having no neighbors within two miles was a selling point for me, but as I park outside and open the door, I realize how damn isolated I am.

Being alone has never worried me before—I've spent a lot of time on my own growing up considering my narcissistic parents cared more about socializing than me—but there's something about this place...a slightly sinister vibe that had been missing when I'd seen it online.

Gritting my teeth against the insane urge to get back in my car, turn around, and head home, I take a few steps toward the front door, determinedly ignoring the frisson of fear snaking down my spine. The porch creaks as I step onto it and the hairs on the back of my neck snap to attention at the sound of a footfall behind me.

My head whips around, but there's no-one. I shove the key labeled 'front door' into the lock as fast as I can regardless, relieved when it turns first try. The door opens soundlessly, and I cross the threshold, unable to see much in the thick darkness. I tap the torch icon on my cell, illuminating a hallway and a living room.

And a hooded figure that opens its mouth and screams.

RYLEE

NOW

The first time Gran took me into town, I'd been a wide-eyed four-year-old who thought Edgewater Bay was the biggest city in the world. I remember the riotous colors—magenta, orange, daffodil—of flowers spilling out of terracotta pots on the sidewalk in front of shops, the salty smell of the sea mingling with frying onions from a hotdog vendor on the oceanfront, the quaintness of a town square with lush lawn and a sparkling white gazebo. It had been picture perfect and from that moment, I'd bug Gran or Dad to take me into town.

But my father rarely left the house and Gran's trips to town were quick—grocery runs or visiting friends—and she rarely let me tag along. As I grew older, I begged them to let me attend the local high school, a red brick building that sprawled over three blocks, but Gran insisted on homeschooling because she needed help with running The

Haven and said I'd learn a lot more through real life experience with people from all walks of life than anything I could absorb in a classroom.

She didn't understand my need for interaction with kids my age, my thirst for friendship. I craved it so badly that I started sneaking out at night, but the furthest I ever got was our neighbor's place before Maisey brought me home. Everyone was petrified of Maisey, a self-proclaimed witch and renowned town kook, but she was the first friend I made outside of The Haven.

She didn't tell Gran about my nocturnal wanderings, as long as I promised not to hitch a ride into town at night, a fair compromise at the time for a fourteen-year-old who was slightly terrified of what Gran might do.

Since that first night I snuck out, I did it a handful of other times, mostly on full moons because that's when Maisey would perform her rituals involving crystals and dancing. She fascinated me, with her serene aura—her words, not mine—the way she talked about magic as if it was every day, and her belief in a goddess. But what I liked most about her was how she treated me like an adult, a person capable of having independent thoughts. Heady stuff, considering my dad and Gran doted on me and insisted on chocolate chip pancakes every Sunday and pot roast on Mondays, because that's what we'd done since I was a kid.

They mean well and I love them, but being sheltered my entire life has fueled my wanderlust. For now, I make do with grocery shopping for Gran and volunteering to head into town whenever anything needs picking up. But the time is fast approaching when I'll leave The Haven; hopefully, to go in search of my mother.

I'd been shattered when Maisey moved into town about

two years ago. I didn't have a cell back then so couldn't text her whenever I felt like it and I knew Gran monitored my emails from the computer we all shared, so we couldn't communicate that way either. I saw her in passing over the last few years if I accompanied Gran into town, but I caught Gran's disapproving frown every time I waved at Maisey and heard Gran muttering 'crazy old bat' so I didn't mention our friendship.

But Maisey isn't crazy. Our conversations had been lucid and enlightening, and I hate how people dismiss or judge things they don't understand.

Today is the first time I've been into town since I graduated—online, of course, so no cap and gown or party for me—and I'm going to seek out Maisey. I miss her. Besides, it can't hurt to ask if she has a spell or charm to manifest a connection with my mom. Not that I believe in it, but I know Maisey will be a good sounding board when I tell her my hopes. Even as a fourteen-year-old, she'd never dismissed me. She'd listened, truly listened, when I'd offloaded about having no friends and feeling like a freak for leading such a sheltered existence.

I know she lives in an apartment above a Wiccan shop. It's obvious when she named her shop *Maisey's Marvels*. The windows are shrouded in black satin, with raindrop shaped crystals hanging by invisible wire of varying lengths, giving the illusion of suspension. It's mystical and alluring, and I can't wait to set foot inside.

I park at the front and kill the engine, eternally grateful that Gran's overprotectiveness didn't extend to me getting a license. She'd even bought me a car, a small SUV, and I treasured the freedom it gave me, even if I've never been further than Edgewater Bay. I know why she'd done it. Dad had convinced her after he'd needed to see the doc in town, and she'd been busy with a social worker appointment for one of our live-ins. The thing is, Dad had winked at me when I'd dropped him at the doctor's office and said he'd see me in an hour, which I took to mean he never had an appointment.

Dad is cool like that. He'd insisted I have a cell for safety once I got my license too. The thought of leaving The Haven might give him anxiety, but he's intuitive enough to realize I'm growing up and I want more.

As I near the door, I see the 'closed' sign has been flipped and my heart sinks. A flimsy purple chiffon drapes the inside of the door and I cup my hands against the glass and peer inside, hoping for a glimpse of movement. There's a flicker to my right, but before I can distinguish what it is, the door flies open and I stumble.

"Rylee?" Maisey's smile is wide, her joy genuine as she pulls me in for a hug. "It's good to see you."

The sting of tears burning my eyes surprises me and I blink them away, mumbling, "Good to see you too," as she releases me.

"Come in." She holds the door open and beckons me inside. "I'm closed to customers for thirty minutes because I've got a potion steeping, but you're welcome anytime."

I follow her into the shop, the heady aroma of sage reminiscent of the times I spent at her house. I'm not sure where to look first. The walls are lined with shelves covered in candles, altar boards, ritual cauldrons, incense and burners, oils in ornate glass bottles every color of the rainbow, sachets of herbs, runes, and various astrology trinkets. Wind chimes and sun catchers hang from the ceiling, and decks of tarot cards are stacked behind the glass counter, along with crystals of every shape and color. Some are familiar—obsidian, rose quartz, citrine, jasper—and I long to pick them up and cradle them in my palm like I used to.

It's a virtual treasure trove of mystic and I could easily spend all day here exploring.

"This is amazing, Maisey." I spin a slow three-sixty, wishing I'd been able to visit sooner.

"I love it," she says, with a shrug. "I don't get a lot of locals stopping by, but the tourists exploring the Outer Banks provide a steady business."

I want to say the locals are a bunch of narrow-minded bigots, but I'd mentioned it once, when I asked if she'd heard the rumors about inhabitants thinking she was crazy, and she'd laughed it off, telling me not to believe in negativity because it can manifest.

"What brings you by?"

Typical Maisey, to act like it's been a week since she last saw me, and not two years. Back then, she never badgered or pushed for answers, preferring to let me do all the talking and interceding when necessary.

"I missed you."

Her smile is soft and understanding. "I've been here since I moved into town, but I'm guessing your grandmother has kept you under lock and key until you've finished your schooling. Correct?"

I nod. "You know what she's like."

Because I'd told her at length, rallying against the injustice of being homeschooled and under the ever-watchful eye of my grandmother.

"How is she these days?"

"Good. The same. Out to save the world and everyone in it."

It's one of the things I admire most about her, but I wish she wasn't so intense all the time.

"With Arcania coming on the market, I'm sure her focus must be elsewhere. Perhaps she has thoughts of expanding The Haven and buying it?"

"What's Arcania?"

Maisey's eyebrows rise. "She's never mentioned it?"

I shake my head.

"It's a huge gothic mansion in Flotilla Firth, almost halfway between here and Nag's Head. Your gran used to work there and was obsessed with the place."

Gran worked? Apart from the altruistic stuff she does at The Haven, I thought Gran hasn't worked a day in her life. She's rich, courtesy of a trust fund set up by her parents, who she refuses to talk about no matter how many times I ask.

"I didn't know she worked there."

"She started not long after she arrived in town. She moved into Oceanview Drive and let people stay at The Haven pretty early on, but I know she worked there because one of my clients recognized her. Said she'd worked along-side Leah in the orchard for months, that your gran couldn't shut up about how much she loved the place. That she arrived early and stayed late, like she never wanted to leave. I'm surprised she's never mentioned it to you?"

I'm not. Gran is introverted and rarely volunteers infor-mation. I know next to nothing about her life before Dad showed up on her doorstep. Heck, I've only just learned about my mom and that's only because I wouldn't let it go like I have in the past.

"She's never said anything about Arcania."

An odd shadow clouds Maisey's eyes. "Maybe she didn't want to dredge up the past."

"Why?"

"Rumors abound at Arcania. Disappearances of workers, the owners dying in an explosion, their son falling down the stairs to his death, then their granddaughter being taken by an alligator..." She shakes her head. "Arcania is shrouded in death."

A shiver tiptoes down my spine, and my skin erupts in goosebumps. I can't imagine Gran anywhere near a place like that, let alone working there. It's bizarre. Yet another mystery to solve.

Maisey gives a little shake. "Anyway, why don't you come through to the back and I'll make us a detox tea?"

"Sounds good."

The familiarity of Maisey's detox tea—juniper berries, lemongrass, ginger, fennel, marigold—is as comforting as the sage permeating the air, and as I settle into a comfy armchair and we catch up, I can't help but wish I shared the same easy-going relationship with my grandmother.

LEAH

THEN

The high-pitched scream pierces my eardrums, so the shadowed figure brandishing what looks like a knife at me is female. It only makes me slightly less terrified. But I've done karate for years—much to my mom's disgust, who tried to railroad me into ballroom dancing instead—and reckon I can hold my own against another woman, even though the thought of trying out the knife-disarming techniques I'd learned is making me want to flee rather than fight.

I flick the nearest light switch as I say, "Who are you and what are you doing in my house?"

As light floods the living room, I see a girl about my age, a foot shorter than me, wrapped in a threadbare blanket. Her brown hair is in pigtails, the freckles dusting her nose stark against her pallor. And the knife I thought she had is, in fact, a rolling pin.

"This isn't your house," she mutters, her top lip curling into a sneer. "I've lived here for months and I've never seen you around town."

I admire her feistiness, but not enough to waste time having a long conversation when all I crave is a shower and bed. "By living here, you mean squatting, right?"

Anger flushes her cheeks. "My mom died and my step-father is a creep, and this place has been empty for over a year, so I thought it'd be okay to *live* here."

I bite back a grin I know she won't appreciate. She's a fighter and I can't help but see a glimpse of myself in her. Sounds like we've both been dealt a bum hand in the parenting stakes and will do whatever it takes to escape.

"You're local?"

She shakes her head. "I'm from Nag's Head, about two hours from here. But I liked the look of Edgewater Bay when I got off the bus, so I stayed."

"Are you in hiding?"

The last thing I need is her deranged stepfather arriving on my doorstep with a vendetta against whoever is harboring her.

"Nope. He doesn't care about me." She spat the word 'he' like a nasty four-letter word. "He got Mom's house and all her stuff, so he'll find someone else to harass now I'm gone."

I glimpse the slightest wobble of her bottom lip when she said mom and my indignation at finding a stranger in my house wanes. Where would I be if I didn't have money? Probably in the same position as this girl, struggling to keep a roof over my head and terrified of ending up on the streets.

I know I'm luckier than most teens who find themselves without a support system. Not that I'll advertise how loaded I am, but this house is huge, and it won't hurt to offer her a room for the night. Besides, I won't mind the company considering the eerie vibes I got earlier.

"Why are you sleeping in the living room and not in one of the bedrooms?"

Her nose crinkles. "Because it wouldn't be right. I've got this blanket," she shrugs it off and I'm surprised it doesn't fall apart it's that thin, "and my backpack as a pillow, so I'm set."

"Would you like a bedroom?"

Her eyes widen before she takes a step back, like she thinks I'm going to barge across the living room and physically drag her upstairs.

"Why would you ask me that?" Her chin juts. "I can't pay you. And besides, I don't need your folks giving me grief and kicking me out tomorrow when they discover their kid has invited a stranger to stay."

She crosses her arms, radiating belligerence. But I glimpse the wariness mingling with fear in her eyes. She doesn't trust anyone, and I don't blame her. As I know too well, even those closest to us can let us down in the worst possible way.

"This is my house," I say. "No parents, just me."

She snorts. "Yeah, right. What are you, nineteen? Twenty tops? And you can afford a place like this?" Her laughter is harsh. "I may be homeless, but I'm not stupid."

I'm glad she's questioning me. It means she's not gullible. I don't know this girl, but to have nobody to rely on so young...I know the feeling.

"I'm eighteen. And I blackmailed my parents into giving me access to my trust fund early because I got sick of their BS and they did something unforgivable." I sweep my arm wide. "So I ditched them, bought this, traveled as far as humanly possible to get away from them, and here I am."

I hold my palms out like I have nothing to hide. "My offer is genuine. If you want a place to stay, choose any bedroom apart from the master, because that's mine. They should all be clean and fully stocked because I got the realtor to call in a cleaning crew and a housekeeper to get everything ready."

"I thought the place smelled different when I got home yesterday." Her eyebrows rise. "You're my age, you own this place, and you're going to live here on your own?"

"I won't be on my own. You'll be staying."

Her eyes narrow, but for the first time since we met, I glimpse hope. "You're not some lunatic, are you?"

I chuckle and hold up my hands. "Nope. Perfectly sane. Nothing to hide."

"This is weird," she mutters, but the corners of her mouth curve upward. "I guess if we're going to be roomies, I should introduce myself. I'm Mel."

"Leah." I point to the front door. "I'll get my things, then I'm going to crash. It's been a long drive."

"Okay." She hesitates. "Can I ask you something?"

"Sure."

"Did the realtor give you the history of this place before you bought it?"

I shake my head. "I was desperate to leave home and have loved the Outer Banks since I was a kid, so when I started searching online, this place popped up at a bargain price. I liked the look of it and the location, so I bought it."

She gnaws on her bottom lip, worry creasing her brow. "This may sound crazy, but I think it's haunted."

"A few ghosts won't scare me." I don't tell her I picked

up on a creepy vibe before I entered. "Why? Has stuff happened while you've been staying here?"

Her lips compress, like she's reluctant to speak, but before I can ask anything else, the front door slams and we jump.

Her gaze is fearful as she stares over my shoulder, and a shiver of foreboding tickles my spine as I turn to see what she's looking at.

I don't know whether to be relieved or terrified when I see nothing at all.

CHAPTER
SEVEN

RYLEE

NOW

Before I head home, I stop by the library. It's silly, sneaking around at eighteen because I don't want my grandmother discovering what I'm researching, but I'd rather be armed with information when I ask her about Arcania than her being forewarned if she checks the search engine on our home computer. Same with my cell, because even though I only recently got it, Gran pays for the plan and I wouldn't put it past her to check up on me somehow. I've disabled the tracking software on it, but Gran's wily and I know she worries about me even though I'm old enough to look after myself.

Heck, I'm the same age she was when she left home and arrived here. And I've never given her any reason to not trust me. But she has this way of watching me when she thinks I'm not looking, part-possessive, part-terror, like she thinks I'll vanish at any second. It's disarming and annoying.

The library is deserted, bar a group of toddlers and their moms having a story time in the kids' corner. The two librarians—a septuagenarian wearing a white maxi dress and crimson glasses, and a thirty-something hipster dude— don't know me. Why would they, when I've only been in here once before about ten years ago when I badgered Gran to see the books my online tutor was talking about? Gran ordered any books I wanted online and most of my school texts were digital, so library visits weren't high on her agenda.

The hipster gives me a nod in greeting as I make my way to computers lining an entire wall. The view is spectacular, overlooking a rolling green hill leading to the ocean, and I experience a pang of regret that I never got to study here so I could be distracted by the vista.

I choose the last carrel and type 'Arcania, Flotilla Firth' into the search engine. The first hit that pops up is a website for the place itself and I click on it, surprised to see it's a wellness center for those wanting to digitally detox. Their emblem is a funky turquoise compass and a photo of the mansion definitely gives off gothic vibes. Emblazoned across the top of the page in red is "UNDER NEW MANAGEMENT."

Maybe Maisey's confused and Arcania has already been sold? As to why she thinks Gran's so obsessed with the place she'd consider buying it...it's unfathomable. Not that Gran couldn't afford it, but why would she take on a wellness retreat? Though Maisey had mentioned Gran expanding The Haven and a mansion of Arcania's size could certainly do that.

I check out a few more links, mostly linking Arcania to

sunken treasure, and a few small news articles on the disappearances and deaths Maisey mentioned. The link at the bottom of the page takes me to a realtor's site, and that's where I see the listing.

Maisey is right. Arcania is for sale. Price on application, which means it'll sell for a squillion.

I take a snapshot of the page with my cell. Time to ask Gran some questions.

But first, I have another stop to make before heading home.

The law firm in town.

EIGHT

LEAH

THEN

T he first night in my new house passes uneventfully. I never found out what spooked Mel after the door slamming incident, because she dismissed my question with a 'I'm tired, thanks for letting me stay, see you in the morning' before bolting upstairs.

Maybe I'd been too tired to care about ghosts or spirits or whatever Mel thinks is haunting this place, but I'd fallen into an exhausted sleep and hadn't stirred until an hour ago.

In daylight, the master bedroom appears stark. Unadorned wooden floors, ecru painted dresser and matching side tables and headboard, khaki coverlet, and no pictures on the walls. It's a serviceable room rather than welcoming, but I don't care. I can spruce it up because it's *mine*.

A small part of me still can't believe my parents gave in

to my demands and let me go so easily. It's clear where their priorities lie: image over parenting. What others think of them is more important than their daughter, and I'll never forgive them.

But they're my past and I need to focus on my future. I won't go to college this year and I doubt I'll ever go. I've never been a brilliant scholar despite the many tutors foisted on me from junior high onwards. Being financially secure gives me options beyond academia, and I'm grateful. At least my folks did one thing right.

Eager to explore, I shrug into a jacket and open my bedroom door to find Mel on the other side with her fist raised, about to knock.

"Hey. Sleep well?"

She nods, but I see the purplish shadows underscoring her eyes. "You?"

"Best sleep I've had in ages."

Her eyebrow arches like she's doubting the validity of that statement. "You didn't hear it?"

"Hear what?"

"A high-pitched screeching." Her gaze darts away. "Probably an owl. Don't worry about it."

I refrain from correcting her, that owls hoot and rarely screech. I'm too practical to believe in ghosts, but there were kids at my high school who devoured paranormal novels by the truckload and would share their theories about otherworldly stuff. Living on my own for the foreseeable future makes me glad I'm a skeptic, but I don't want to dismiss Mel or make light of what she thinks.

"You asked me last night if I knew the history of this place before I bought it. I don't, but what have you heard?"

Her stomach rumbles loudly and before she can answer, I say, "You can tell me over breakfast."

Her eyes light up for the first time since we met last night. "I'm starving."

Sadly, I think she means it literally, considering she's been squatting here and appears thin to the point of emaciation.

"I brought the basics with me last night and the fridge should be stocked, so what do you feel like?"

"Anything," she says, falling into step beside me as we descend the stairs.

I can't deny the house is gloomy. Even with the bright sunshine streaming through my bedroom window when I opened the curtains earlier, it hadn't dispelled the shadows completely, and it looks like the rest of the house is worse.

The ceilings are lower than they appeared in the photos online and the dark wood paneling that lines the walls accentuates the closed in feeling. The floors are redwood and the sconces lining the hallway are pretty, but there's an oppressiveness I can't shake as we enter the kitchen.

Apart from the location, this is the room that drew me to the house. It's massive and modern, with a gleaming marble topped island bench lined with six bar stools, an eight-seat pine dining table in one corner, a giant walk-in pantry, and trendy gray cupboards with matching counter-tops. It gives off a welcoming vibe and is the complete antithesis of my kitchen back home, and the rest of the house.

I can see myself spending a lot of time in here. Not that I enjoy cooking, per se, but being left to fend for myself most of the time growing up means I know my way around a kitchen. I hated the pre-prepared healthy meals Mom stocked the fridge with so I wouldn't put on weight—thanks for the body issues, Mom—and I'd often open the packaging and tip the contents in the trash before making myself macaroni and cheese.

"This is my favorite room in the house," Mel murmurs, and I flash her an understanding smile.

"Me too. The moment I saw the photos online, I knew I wanted to live here." I cross to the fridge and open it, grateful the realtor has followed my instructions to the letter and hired a competent housekeeper to prepare for my arrival. "How about eggs and bacon with toast, and OJ?"

"Sounds amazing. What can I do?"

"There should be a loaf of bread in the pantry, so you can make the toast."

"Done."

I feel like I'm in a dream as I add bacon to one pan and crack eggs into another, a dream where I'm free of expectations and judgement, a dream I never want to wake from.

"What are you smiling at?" Mel places two plates of buttered toast on the countertop next to the stove.

"I guess I'm happy for the first time in a long time," I say, topping the toast with the eggs and bacon. "It's weird to be living on my own and I like it."

She hesitates before nodding. "It gets lonely sometimes. I mean, I'd much rather be here than with my sleazy stepfather, and I've made some friends in town, but having nobody to rely on..."

I see the sadness in her eyes as she trails off and I reach out to give her arm an impulsive squeeze. "Hey, you've got me now, and you can stay here as long as you like."

She lets my hand linger a moment before shrugging it off, her defiance returning. "I appreciate you being so nice, but I know that nobody does anything without expecting something in return and I don't understand what your angle is."

I understand her cynicism. Girls our age on our own have to be.

"No angle." I pick up the plates and head to the dining table, where she's set places for us. "This is a big house. I'm lucky enough to have money. And I get lonely too, so you'll be doing me a favor by sticking around."

She rolls her eyes, but she smiles. "Don't expect us to be friends. We're too different."

"I wouldn't dare," I say, and she laughs at my droll response. "Now, let's eat. Then you can tell me what you know about the history of this house."

We eat in companionable silence, though by the way Mel shovels the food into her mouth, I assume it's been a long while since she's had a decent meal. She probably had some savings when she ran away, but if she's been here for months, I'd hazard a guess she's in dire need of funds.

"Are you working?"

She nods and waits until she finishes chewing before responding. "There's a fish co-op in town that always needs extra hands when the boats come in. It's casual work and minimum wage, but beggars can't be choosers."

I see the judgement in her eyes that I'm one of the lucky ones. I know I am. To be totally free from my past is liberating. And it's in this moment, with this feisty, self-sufficient young woman almost taunting me for having it easy with my wealth, I decide to do something proactive with it.

"Do you know of other teens who need a place to stay?"

Her eyes narrow, suspicious. "One or two I've met. Why?"

"Because this place is enormous, and it seems wrong to have all these empty rooms when people need somewhere to sleep."

She's staring at me like she can't quite figure me out as

she places her cutlery neatly on her empty plate. "You know nothing about these homeless kids. They could rob you blind. Or worse."

I don't say that being forced to give up my child for adoption, only to have it die, has been rock-bottom for me and nothing a few teens dish out can make things worse.

I shrug. "The offer stands. I know I'm lucky and I want to help. That's it. No ulterior motive."

Our gazes lock and she must see the honesty in mine because she eventually smiles. "I'm heading into town now for a shift, so I'll let them know."

As I clear the dishes, Mel adds, "Thanks, Leah. There aren't many good people in this world, but you're one of them."

I turn away so she doesn't see the tears pooling in my eyes. I blink them away because I've cried enough: for my baby, for my parents, for my life as I knew it.

It isn't until Mel leaves do I remember she hasn't told me the history of this house.

RYLEE

NOW

The offices of *Mackay and Son* are a short stroll from the library. Dad inadvertently put the idea of visiting the lawyers into my head when I asked him about Mom, and he mentioned they'd had wills drawn up when she discovered she was pregnant. Gran had insisted on it, apparently. Considering her fortune, I don't blame her. If something happened to her and Dad, I would've inherited everything, but Mom would've been in control of it and Gran would've wanted to protect my inheritance. Considering Mom absconded, with good reason.

Dad said it gave him hope initially that Mom would return because he'd never been contacted by the lawyers to inform him of her death, but as the years went by, he accepted she'd never come back.

It made me wonder though. If Mom had arrived at The

Haven in search of refuge, that meant she'd been fleeing from something or someone and had little savings. Which also meant a cushy life with my dad, and the backing of Gran's money, would've been an excellent incentive to stick around. So either she really hated the sight of me at birth and couldn't get away fast enough, or she'd been driven away by personal demons. The sentimental optimist in me hopes it's the latter, because if I go to all the trouble of finding her now and she still doesn't want me, I'll be shattered.

The receptionist's desk is empty when I enter the lawyer's office and the place is deserted, but there's a partially open door with "Barry Mackay" on the brass nameplate and I hear a gruff voice barking orders about escrow followed by the slam of a phone.

"Hello?" I call out, wishing I'd made an appointment when a towering giant of a man wearing an ill-fitting navy suit and a permanent frown yanks open his door and glowers at me.

"I don't have anyone booked for another hour. Who are you?"

I flash a smile and hold out my hand. "Rylee Smith. I was hoping I could have a few moments of your time."

"Barry Mackay." His frown eases as he shakes my hand. "I've been expecting you."

He has? My confusion must show because he gestures at his office. "Come in and we can discuss it."

I follow him into his cavernous office. A huge mahogany desk dominates the room, and the walls are lined with ancient books that appear to weigh at least ten pounds each. Light streams in through a wall-to-wall window, highlighting the dancing dust motes as he sits behind his desk and points to the chair opposite.

"Did your father or grandmother send you?"

I shake my head. "They don't know I'm here. Dad mentioned he and my mom made wills with you before I was born, and now that I'm looking for her, I thought this might be a place to start. She might've left a forwarding address when she left?"

It's a long shot and highly doubtful, because this would be the first place Gran and Dad looked if they wanted to find her, but I have to say something other than 'I'm desperate and hope you can give me some clue to her whereabouts.'

"Good. Let's keep it that way." He clears his throat. "Your mother insisted on it."

A flicker of hope unfurls in my heart. "Do you know where she is?"

"No. But she made it clear her letters to you were to remain a secret and if you ever showed up here once you were eighteen that I insisted on your discretion before I give them to you."

"Letters?"

I sound like an idiot parroting him, but my gut is churning with a mix of excitement and trepidation. My mom has reached out to me, but she wants it to be a secret, which can only mean one thing.

She fled because of something my father or grandmother did.

"Your mother has been sending a letter to this office every year on your birthday, with explicit instructions to give them to you if you should ever come here in search of her after you turned eighteen, which you have." He steeples his fingers together. "And I can only assume her stipulation about keeping them private comes from a place of concern for you. Do you agree?"

I nod, speechless at the thought of discovering a connection with my mother. She hadn't forgotten me despite all indications to the contrary and depending on what's in the letters, maybe I can find her sooner rather than later?

"Do you have an address for her?"

"No. And oddly, no letter arrived on your eighteenth birthday."

Dread settles in the pit of my stomach. Has something happened to her?

"Then again, mail can be unreliable, and it may have gone astray, so I'll let you know if it turns up." He stands. "Wait one moment while I get the letters."

My mind spins as he leaves the office. I have so many questions and hopefully, my mother will answer them in her letters. I should be angry at her subterfuge. What would've happened if I'd never come to this office in search of some hint of her whereabouts? Would I be clueless regarding her intentions of leaving me? Would I have spent my life thinking I'm flawed somehow, that I'm not good enough?

Barry strides back into the office and places a pile of letters secured by an elastic band in front of me. The envelopes are white, plain, nondescript, with the lawyer's address typed rather than handwritten.

"Here you go. Is there anything else I can help you with?"

I stare at the letters like they'll combust if I touch them, equal parts hopeful and terrified of the contents. "One question. What would've happened to the letters if I hadn't shown up?"

"They would've remained here. Your mother made it

clear she only wanted you to have them if you came in search of her."

"Okay, thanks." I stand and pick up the letters. "Did she leave anything else for me? Anything at all?"

Pity gleams in his eyes for a moment before his professional mask slides back into place. "No, I'm sorry. The letters are the only thing she left for you."

I should be grateful I have these, proof she's alive and wants to establish some kind of contact with me. But the kernel of resentment that's resided within me my entire life is hard to ignore. No matter what she's revealed in these letters, they can't make up for her absenteeism for whatever reason.

"Thanks again," I say, and shove the letters into my bag, hoping I'll finally get the answers I crave once I read them.

TEN

LEAH

THEN

After Mel leaves, I explore. The house is in pristine condition thanks to the money I threw at the realtor to have everything ready—lightbulbs changed, lawns mowed, cobwebs removed. Even the shed in the backyard that stores gardening equipment and old pieces of furniture is clean. Everything is stacked neatly, with tools clearly labeled, which is why the sign stands out.

It's ancient, a rotting piece of wood that looks like a plank pried off an old shipwreck, with *The Haven* crudely burned into the wood. The sign is propped on an angle between a broom and rake, like it's been flung haphazardly and is about to topple at any second.

The Haven. Is that the name of the house? If so, it's a tad creepy, as that's exactly what I'm offering Mel and her homeless friends. A haven. A sanctuary. A place to feel safe.

Has the house been used similarly in the past? If so, the

coincidence is uncanny. I'd been too exhausted last night to do an online search on this address, and Mel still hasn't told me the supposed history, but with a name now I slide my cell out of my pocket and bring up a search engine.

I type 'The Haven, Edgewater Bay' and hit search. Nothing. Not a single hit. So I broaden it to 'haunted houses in Edgewater Bay.' Still nothing. I'm not sure whether to be relieved or annoyed. I'm glad my new house doesn't have ghosts, but that means the overall feel I got last night, that something isn't quite right, is in my imagination.

Mel saying it has a haunted history didn't help and when she gets back later today, I'll ask her what she knows, but for now I'm going to hang the sign above the front door and then hit the road. I remember an incredible Farmers Market in Nag's Head that I visited with my parents years ago and I'm keen to stock up on produce. If Mel looks like she could do with a hearty meal I'm assuming her friend will too if they've been homeless for a while.

Almost two hours later, after an exhilarating drive along a gorgeous coastline, I enter the market. It hasn't changed in a decade. The sugary aroma of candy floss and the spicy fragrance of pork ribs in a smoker is heavy in the air and my mouth waters as I stroll past the stalls featuring homemade jellies, cookies, hand poured soy candles, knitted scarves, and fruits and vegetables in crates. It's not too busy and I take my time exploring, trying not to pinch myself to check this isn't a dream.

Last week I'd been in hospital under the watchful eye of my parents, having my soul ripped out. I don't want to think about what I did, giving in to them, and the resultant pain I'll have to live with for the rest of my life.

They did this to me.

Cutting them off is the best thing I could've done, but it

doesn't change facts: thanks to them, I'll never have children.

The pain that stabs my heart is swift and sharp and unexpected. So much for having a grip on my emotions. And I don't know I'm crying until a gentle hand lands on my shoulder and a deep voice says, "Hey. Are you okay?"

I blink the blurriness away and stifle a gasp as I look at the guy who's been kind enough to check if I'm all right.

He's gorgeous.

Dark brown curls the color of my favorite chocolate, high cheekbones, square jaw dusted in stubble, and hazel eyes with a wicked gleam like he knows something I don't. When his lips ease into a lazy smile, I struggle not to gape.

"I'm Spencer. It looks like you could do with a cup of coffee." He points to a food truck. "I was just going to grab one. Want to join me?"

My brain is too befuddled by his gorgeousness for me to answer, but I manage a mute nod and follow him.

"Cream and sugar?" He asks, and I finally get my mouth to work.

"Yes please, one sugar."

He smiles again and I swear my heart stops. My skin flushes and tingles with awareness. I want to touch him, which is ludicrous. I've never had this reaction to any guy before and I can't fathom it.

I didn't date in high school. I was too much of a goody-two-shoes intent on getting good grades in my never-ending quest to not disappoint my parents. My inexperience with guys pretty much explained why I had no clue when the condom broke; or why Chad couldn't get away from me fast enough afterward.

I never told Chad when two blue lines popped up on the pregnancy test. What would be the point? But I had told

Mom because I thought she'd support me, that she'd plead with Dad on my behalf when I wanted to keep my baby.

More fool me.

"Here you go." Spencer hands me a takeout cup and our fingers brush, sending a jolt of heat through me.

I manage a sedate "Thanks," and take a sip before I blurt out the questions pinging through my mind. *Where are you from? How old are you? Would you like my number?*

He raises his cup. "To new friends."

"Are we friends? You don't know me."

The corners of his eyes crinkle adorably when he smiles. "I will if you tell me your name."

"Leah Smith."

"Pleased to meet you, Leah." He taps his cup against mine. "And I'm glad to see you looking happier now." He winks. "There's nothing a good caffeine hit can't cure."

My perkier mood has nothing to do with the excellent coffee and everything to do with Spencer staring at me with blatant interest. Or maybe that's wishful thinking.

I should be embarrassed he caught me crying, but I'm not, because there's something about this guy that makes me want to bury my head in his chest, wrap my arms around his waist, and never let go. Crazy.

"What brings you to the Outer Banks? Are you here on vacation?"

I shake my head. "No, I just moved here."

"Good for you. It's a great place to live. Is your family here?"

It's not smart to divulge too much to a guy I just met, especially that I'm here alone. But his eyes are guileless, and I find myself wanting to tell him everything despite my innate self-preservation mechanism urging me to be cautious.

"It's just me."

His eyebrows rise, but he doesn't call me out for being too young to be on my own. Instead, he gives a brief nod. "It's just me too. Being independent is the best."

"Do you live around here?"

"I live and work at Arcania, about thirty minutes from here."

I've never heard of it, which is unusual considering I studied every town along the entire Outer Banks region when I'd been looking at buying a place.

As if sensing my confusion, he says, "Arcania's an organic farm where I work, in the small town of Flotilla Firth. If you're looking for a job, I can put in a good word for you..."

He trails off as a red convertible pulls up near us and a handsome guy in khaki chinos and a white polo shirt gets out, his gaze inscrutable behind designer shades as he looks around before striding toward one of the stalls.

When I look back at Spencer, he's scowling, and a deep frown is grooving his brow.

"Do you know that guy?"

"Yeah. Harlan Medville. He's the son of Arcania's owners."

"So he's your boss?"

"Something like that."

If looks could kill, Harlan's back would be sporting twenty knives.

"You don't like him?"

Spencer smiles, but it's forced. "I don't like what he stands for. Never had to work a day in his life. Gifted everything from Mommy and Daddy. One of those trust fund kids who swans around like he can buy anything and anybody."

I stiffen. What would Spencer think of me if he knew I'm one of those trust fund kids he loathes?

I'd been about to tell him I was lucky enough not to need to work when he'd offered me a job a few minutes ago, but now I know I need to keep my mouth shut.

It's stupid to indulge my first full-blown crush when I barely knew this guy, but I've never felt this way before, and I want to explore it.

"You mentioned a job at Arcania?"

His eyes light up. "Yeah. They hire people like us all the time, so why don't you follow me back there now?"

By 'people like us' I assume he means loners, but I don't question him.

Instead, I ignore my voice of reason insisting this is ridiculous, shelve my common sense, and follow him to Arcania.

ELEVEN

RYLEE

NOW

When I get back to The Haven, I'm dying to read Mom's letters. But first I need to unpack the groceries. Gran's in the kitchen, whipping up a batch of her mini quiches, and I paste a sunny smile on my face to hide the many questions swirling through my head.

Are you obsessed with Arcania?

Did you ever work there?

What is Maisey talking about?

Did you have something to do with Mom leaving?

I hate doubting my Gran because she's been my rock forever, though the fact my mother went to great lengths to keep her letters to me a secret implies either Gran or Dad had something to do with her fleeing. Considering how docile my dad is, I can't see him being the cause.

"How was your trip into town?" Gran opens the oven door and slides the last batch of quiches in.

"Good. The usual." I hoist four reusable mesh bags onto the counter and start unloading the vegetables and fruit.

I may be okay at keeping my expression neutral, but she must hear something in my tone because she pins me with a narrow-eyed stare.

"What happened?"

"Nothing," I say too quickly, and she lets out a hefty sigh.

"Don't lie to me, young lady."

I bark out a laugh because it's the same admonishment she's used forever. Not that I'm in the habit of lying to my grandmother, but any time she suspected I was withholding from her, she'd used the same phrase.

"I ran into Maisey."

"That old kook." Gran rolls her eyes. "Is she still terrorizing the town with her hocus pocus nonsense?"

"She's a practicing witch, Gran. Wicca is her religion. You shouldn't dismiss it."

Gran snorts as I open the fridge and stack the bunches of celery and bags of carrots she'll use to make her hearty soup later.

"Each to their own, I suppose," she says, her sniff dismissive.

"Actually, she mentioned you."

Gran stiffens slightly. "What did she say?"

"That you might be interested in buying Arcania, a wellness retreat you worked at years ago."

I watch Gran closely for the slightest reaction and when she blanches, I know Maisey's ramblings aren't far off the mark.

"I've never worked at a wellness retreat," she says, her

tone derisive. "You know I've always had a trust fund, so why would I need to work?"

Gran's lying.

I see it in her evasive glance, in the way her fingers grip the edge of the counter, so hard her knuckles stand out.

"So you know nothing about Arcania?"

She frowns and shoots me a warning glare. "At the risk of repeating myself, Rylee, I've never worked at a wellness retreat."

It's not lost on me she hasn't answered my question about Arcania but has merely reiterated not working there.

"Maisey must be mistaken," I say, but Gran hasn't lost the worried expression or rigid posture.

Dad strolls into the kitchen and plucks an apple from the fruit bowl. "What's Maisey mistaken about?"

"Nothing," Gran almost yells, a second before I say, "She thought Gran worked at a wellness retreat years ago."

Dad laughs. "Your grandmother hasn't worked a day in her life." Seeing her glower, he adds, "Apart from the never-ending work involved in running this place, looking after me, and raising you, that is."

He raises the apple. "Thanks, Mom."

Gran softens as she always does whenever Dad calls her Mom. They may not be biologically related, but Dad's life began when he walked into The Haven seeking refuge and he considers Gran his mother in every sense of the word.

"Those groceries won't unpack themselves," Gran says, pointing to the three bags I haven't emptied yet. "And if you could keep an eye on the last batch of quiches, Rylee, I need your father to help me with moving a trellis in the garden."

"No problem," I say, but as Dad crunches into his apple and follows Gran out the back door, I think there is a problem.

What motive does Maisey have for inventing stuff about Gran?

And if she isn't, that means Gran's lying.

Why?

CHAPTER
TWELVE

LEAH

THEN

The moment Spencer's pickup turns into the drive of Arcania and I follow, I break into a cold sweat.

I can't explain it, but it's the same eerie feeling I got when I was in junior high and we visited an old jail; and more recently, last night when I set foot in my new house, but to a lesser degree.

I wasn't lying when I told Mel I don't believe in ghosts and don't spook easily, but as I park behind Spencer and get out of my car, my first glimpse of Arcania results in dread settling in the pit of my stomach.

Spencer waves me over, then points at the mansion. "It's something else, huh?"

"Yeah," I say, trying not to gawp at the creepy facade. About fifteen black-trimmed windows line the top and bottom floors, and the place is painted a dark gray that mimics stormy skies. The ebony double doors match the window trims and from this distance, I'm not sure if the knocker is a gargoyle or the devil.

"I've worked here for two years. Do you need a place to stay too? Because most of the workers live here like me."

I'd like nothing better than to be roomies with Spencer, but I have a new house and boarders to think about. "Thanks, I'm all set with living arrangements."

"Shame. I would've liked to hang out with you after work." He winks again, and I find it endearing rather than sleazy. "Come check out the back."

He leads me along a cracked stone path and I welcome a cool breeze that lifts the hair at my nape. It's bad enough Spencer looks like a bad boy who's stepped from the pages of a romance novel, but he smells great too, a tempting blend of ocean and citrus.

As we round the corner, I spy several large white tents dotting an enormous lawn.

"Couples and families who work here live in the tents. Single folk get to stay in the house. The orchards are just beyond here."

We skirt the tents and enter the orchards. Apples mostly.

"The Medville's grow everything here and are the biggest organic supplier in North Carolina. Workers come and go, so there's a regular turnover, hence they're always on the lookout for new employees." His smile makes my heart flip. "Which is where you come in. Helga's going over accounts today if you want to meet her now for an impromptu interview?"

This is crazy. I don't need a job. I'm flush with funds and will be for the foreseeable future. So why am I contemplating working in an orchard to be close to a crush?

I should leave. Head back to The Haven—I love the

name because that's what it is to me—and start rebuilding my life.

Instead, I return his smile. "Sounds good."

Thirty minutes later, I've had the briefest interview with Helga, who's friendly yet intimidating, and I've got the job. When I exit her office, Spencer is waiting for me and when I tell him, he takes a step toward me and for a heart-stopping moment I think he's going to embrace me.

"Welcome aboard, Leah." He sweeps his arm wide. "Want the grand tour?"

"Sounds good."

As he takes me around, I can't help but wonder why the Medville's run an orchard at all. The mansion is opulent, though heavy on the goth, and the furnishings, paintings, and fixtures are worth a fortune—I can thank Mom for my crash course in antiques several years ago.

"Do you dive?"

Spencer's question is from left field, and I shake my head. "No. Why?"

"Buried treasure, of course." His grin is infectious, like a little boy about to impart a fairytale. "The Medville's Viking ancestors shipwrecked not far off the coast here. Those that survived built this place with the gold they salvaged, but there's plenty more stuck down there, along with a price-less compass the family is obsessed with finding."

He rolls his eyes. "Most workers take it in turns to dive and those who don't know how are offered free lessons to get accredited. It's a big thing around here, the quest to find the compass. You'll see."

I have no intention of taking diving lessons—there's only so far I'll go to indulge my crush and taking a job I don't need is enough. "I don't believe in fairytales."

"Too bad." Spencer leans in close and I inhale softly,

trying to be subtle so he doesn't think I'm a total loon. "I'm always up for rescuing a damsel in distress."

My chuckle is nervous as he straightens. I may not need saving, but if it means spending more time with Spencer, maybe I can fake it.

RYLEE

NOW

Gran and Dad still aren't back when the oven timer dings, so I slide the quiches out of the oven and place them on a cooling rack. I've finished unpacking the groceries, and the kitchen is tidy, so I finally have time to read the letters.

I bolt up the stairs to my room, skipping every second step like I've done since I grew tall enough to do it, around the age of twelve. I love this old house, every creaky, haunted inch of it.

Not that I've ever seen a ghost, but I've felt a presence many times, like the barest brush of fingertips against the nape of my neck. It's not scary, more a reassurance that I'm not alone.

When I was younger, I used to think it was Mom letting me know she was still around, but I didn't like that thought because if she was a ghost that meant she was dead, and I always harbored hope that one day she'd come back.

It's annoying that a chance visit to the family lawyer has resulted in discovering the letters she left for me all these years, but incredible, too. Mom may have left, but she didn't abandon me and the letters prove it. With a little luck, they'll provide me with a way to find her.

The bedroom doors have locks installed by Gran once she started taking people in to give them some security, considering what many ran from, and I've never been more grateful. The last thing I need is Gran or Dad walking in on me.

There's a loose floorboard under my bed and from childhood, I've stored my treasures in a cardboard box covered in cut-out fairies. I made the box with Gran on my seventh birthday and it evokes amazing memories. She'd hired a jumping castle and invited Mel and Freda—her friends—and their children. There'd been cotton candy and popcorn and sodas, and even ponies. It had been magical, but what I'd loved most was the time Gran spent with me that evening making the box.

Gran isn't a patient person. She's a go-getter who gets things done and doesn't have time for apathetic people who won't help themselves. It's why so many of the runaways she takes in leave much stronger, empowered to leave their past behind and embrace the future. And it's why I've always been a tad scared of her. She's intimidating and never put up with my occasional lamenting of not having a mother.

That evening of my seventh birthday is the first time I'd seen my gran so lighthearted, so whimsical. She'd delighted in cutting out the fairies from various gift-wrapping left-overs and pasting them on the box with me. We'd slathered on pink and purple glitter and stuffed our faces with left-over cookies. It's the most relaxed I'd ever seen her.

Now, as I carefully lift the box from the space in the floorboards, I wonder why my gran is lying to me.

Because the more I rehash that scene in the kitchen a while ago, the more convinced I am she's lying about not knowing Arcania. She'd visibly paled when I mentioned it and that's not a normal reaction. And she'd practically hustled Dad out of the kitchen to avoid me asking anything else about it.

There's another way to get answers about Arcania and that's to visit the place. Surely there must be someone who's worked there long enough to know my gran if she had been an employee?

It feels wrong to sneak around behind her back, but I've spent my lifetime being sheltered in this place, and discovering the existence of my mother's letters makes me wonder what else I don't know.

I carefully slide the letters out of my bag, tug the top one out from under the elastic band holding them together, and place the rest in the box. I want to take my time with each letter, savor them, absorb the impact of my mother's words. Besides, if I rush through them, I fear I'll get to the end too quickly and will be none the wiser about her whereabouts, and that will crush me all over again.

I lift the envelope to my nose and sniff. I love the smell of new books and have since I was a kid, but I know why I'm smelling this letter: I hope it may have a fragrance unique to Mom. Silly, because the letter is eighteen years old and has been stored at the lawyer's office with goodness knows however many other documents for that long, but I inhale nonetheless, stifling my disappointment when there's nothing but the faintest hint of mustiness.

The envelope is plain, white, with Rylee printed in block letters on a label that's stuck in the middle. Why wouldn't she just write my name? Unless she didn't want her hand-writing to be recognized on the off-chance Dad or Gran saw the envelope...

Hating the doubts about the only family I've ever known, I slide my finger into the gap at the top of the envelope and make a slashing motion, tearing it open. The faintest scent of vanilla teases my nose as I slide a single sheet of folded paper out of the envelope and tears inexplicably sting my eyes at the thought that could be my mom's fragrance.

My fingers tremble as I unfold the paper and I take a deep breath, exhale, before starting to read.

FOURTEEN

LEAH

THEN

I'm still in a daze several hours later as I stir store-bought pesto into cooked fettuccini and grate parmesan over it. Mel and her friend Freda are washing up and I'm grateful for a few minutes of peace. Mel isn't exactly chatty, but her friend Freda hasn't shut up since they arrived home thirty minutes ago.

Strange, that I already think of The Haven as home when I've been here less than twenty-four hours. I expected to feel more disjointed, transplanting here from Harrisburg, but it's like I've shut off memories of my old life in a quest to embrace my new. Probably a self-preservation mechanism, to keep the grief at losing my baby at bay. That might explain my irrational, instantaneous crush on Spencer too; another coping strategy to obliterate the bad in my life.

The girls are talking about a hot fisherman as they reenter the kitchen. Their giggling is heartwarming and makes me feel like their mother rather than a peer. When's the last time I laughed over anything?

Though Spencer made me smile several times today and I think I chuckled once. He's definitely good for me. I'll have to keep telling myself that when I'm picking apples tomorrow in a repetitive job I don't need.

"Hope you're hungry." I place bowls of steaming pasta in front of the girls and their eyes widen to saucer proportions.

Mel, who demolished the breakfast I made, says "thanks", and picks up her fork before stabbing it into the fettuccini and twirling.

Freda's hesitant, her gaze flicking between the pasta and me, as if she can't quite believe it's real. "When Mel said I could stay here, I couldn't believe my luck. But I didn't expect...I mean, this is great, but..." Her face reddens. "I can't pay you."

My chest clenches at the wariness in her eyes. I hate to think about what she's gone through to end up homeless and distrustful of everyone.

"It's okay, Freda, no payment necessary. My folks may have been jerks, but the one good thing they did was give me enough money to live off. So you can stay here rent free for as long as you like and eat whatever you want. The fridge and pantry will be fully stocked all the time."

She gapes at me, and I flash a reassuring smile. "I expect nothing in return, honest."

Mel finishes chewing before she jabs Freda in the ribs. "See, told you. Leah's like our fairy godmother, except she's our age."

Freda manages a nod, but she still hasn't lost the stunned expression as she tentatively picks up the fork. "Thanks, Leah. This is really nice of you."

"No problem," I say, and we eat in companionable silence, punctuated by the occasional appreciative moan from Freda.

When our bowls are clean, Freda leaps to her feet and starts clearing the dishes. "That was the best pasta I've ever had," she says, patting her stomach.

"Me too," Mel adds, opening the dishwasher, and a strange warmth infuses me at the thought that simple pasta has earned this much gratitude.

I've spent my life taking things for granted, making me more like my parents than I'd like to admit. How many times had I indulged in my favorite lobster mornay rigatoni at Harrisburg's fanciest Italian restaurant, without thinking that it cost more than what these girls probably earned in a week?

I'm spoiled and cosseted and leaving my old life behind is the best thing I've ever done. Working a manual job will be good for me, too. I've already pondered what I can do with my wages and rather than donating to a local charity, perhaps I can ask the girls where they think the money will be best spent.

Mel snaps her fingers. "Hey, I almost forgot. One of the fishermen on the boat today was talking about local myths—"

"He was trying to impress us with spooky stories." Freda rolls her eyes. "We're eighteen, not twelve."

Mel grins. "Anyway, remember I mentioned the history of this place? Well, he's heard the rumors too."

Intrigued, I ladle the leftover pasta into an airtight container and store it in the fridge. "What rumors?"

"Apparently, this house was a haven for lost souls, mainly witches, who sought refuge from those wanting to harm them." Mel wiggles her eyebrows. "I told you it was haunted. Imagine all the spells and ghouls and other-worldly stuff they conjured up here."

Freda snickers. "And if you believe that, you'll believe anything."

I agree with Freda, but before I can tell her, the lights go out and we're plunged into darkness.

Mel screams and Freda groans. "Quit it, Mel. It's just a fuse."

"I'll go check it out," I say, picking up my cell from the bench top and switching on the torch icon.

But when I go outside to the fuse box, everything is in order and when I turn, I swear I see someone watching me from beyond the fence line.

FIFTEEN

RYLEE

NOW

I stop reading at *Dear Rylee*.

Crazy, because I want to devour the letter as fast as humanly possible, but a part of me is terrified that whatever I discover will change my view of the people who matter the most: my father, my grandmother, or my mother.

My fingers convulse and the edges of the letter crumple. This is huge for me, discovering the mother I've always wondered about took the time to reach out annually hoping one day I'd want to know more about her.

I'd be a fool to waste this opportunity.

I smooth the letter against my thigh and start reading again.

Dear Rylee,

By the time you read this, you'll probably hate me. Eighteen years is a long time to believe your mother abandoned you. But that's not true and all I ask is that you take as long as you need to read my letters, in the hope you'll gain some understanding of why I left and the woman I've become.

Firstly, and most importantly, I love you.

I loved you from the moment I discovered I was pregnant, despite being utterly terrified too.

I loved you all those months you grew in my belly.

I loved you from the first moment I held you in my arms.

And I loved you every hour of the ten days I got to spend with you before I had to leave. Note that I had to leave, not wanted to leave, because nothing would've made me abandon you apart from...well, more about that later.

To gain insight into me as a person, let me summarize my life before I arrived at The Haven and met your father. (He's an amazing man and I hope he's well. He had nothing to do with my leaving.)

I came from a wealthy family in Chicago. Had the perfect life really—good grades at an exclusive school, college plans, the best of everything—until my mom died a month before I graduated. We'd never been super close, because I could never forgive her for marrying my asshole stepfather less than a year after my dad died when I was fifteen, but I still grieved her. I resented her too, because it left me alone with him.

I won't go into details, but my stepfather always made my skin crawl. He had this way of looking at me when Mom wasn't around that made me glad to have a lock on my bedroom door. So when Mom passed away, I couldn't bear to be in the house alone with him, so I slept in the cottage with our live-in help, Marta, who'd practically raised me. I'm ashamed to say I exaggerated my grief, but it's the only way I could stay with Marta at night. I knew it wasn't a long-term solution, but I was counting down the days until I graduated.

I could've gone to college, but that would've meant being dependent on him, connected to him, and I wanted to sever ties.

So the day after I graduated, I ran. Packed as many clothes as I could fit into a duffel, hid the cash I'd been withdrawing over the last month, and hopped on a bus. I ended up in Nag's Head, where I heard about a house in Edgewater Bay that took in runaways, so that's how I ended up at The Haven.

Your father and I fell for each other quickly, but we both tried to hide it. Then I had a nightmare one night, and he rushed into my room to comfort me, and that's the night we conceived you.

I'm not sure how close you are to your grandmother, and I hate to disillusion you if you think she's the greatest person, but for you to understand me, you need to know the truth, however painful it is.

I'm sorry, sweetheart, if this hurts you, but you need to know.

Your grandmother hated me from the start. Then again, she would've hated anyone who ventured near your father. She had an odd possessiveness, almost like she feared losing him if she loosened the apron strings. When she heard I was pregnant, I've never seen that much banked rage in a person's eyes. She pretended to support us, faked it for your father's sake, but I didn't trust her.

In the end, I was right not to.

From the moment you were born, her possessiveness of your father extended to you. She coveted you to the extent it creeped me out. I confronted her, and she snapped. She said you were the baby she never had, that she'd do a better job raising you, and if I didn't leave, she wouldn't be responsible for her actions.

Rylee, I was terrified. I made plans with your father to leave, the three of us. I didn't have much money left by that stage and your father depended solely on Leah financially, but I was desperate to get away.

I don't know how, but Leah found out. When your father took you for a walk, she cornered me and threatened me. That if I didn't leave, she'd take me to court and I'd lose custody. That she'd make sure of it. That she'd do whatever it took. She blackmailed me about something I'd done in my past which I won't go into now, but I was frightened for my life, but I knew she'd never harm you. So I left. I took the money she gave me, twenty thousand dollars, to stay away.

I know it appears like a callous decision, Rylee, but you don't know your grandmother. At least, I hope you don't. I know you've been raised in a loving household because one of Leah's friends, Freda, has kept me informed over the years, at substantial risk to herself. But getting her updates is the only way I've been able to stay away and not go insane, wondering if I made the right decision leaving you behind.

Because I contemplated taking you with me, but how far would a twenty-two-year-old single mom runaway with a baby have got? Leah would've done everything she could to find us and when she did, I have no doubt she would've had me locked up or worse.

Freda knows about these letters, but I swore her to secrecy, because I wanted you to make the first move to reach out and get to know me. Please don't blame her for keeping my confidence.

And if, by the end of reading all the letters you want to meet me, I would love nothing more.

I love you, Rylee.

Always have.

I hope you can forgive me for leaving.

Love,

Mom xx

. . .

TEARS ARE STREAMING DOWN my face and I'm unaware until one plops onto the page and leaves a smear. I swipe them away and press my mother's letter to my chest, before starting to read it again.

There's a lot to absorb. I don't know if I can forgive her, but I want to know her.

And I need to figure out what the hell is my grandmother's problem.

SIXTEEN

LEAH

THEN

O ver the next few weeks, I fall into a routine. Up at dawn for breakfast with the girls, then we go our separate ways to work. Mel and Freda think it's hilarious I'm working at Arcania when I don't have to, until I tell them they can choose whatever cause can use the money and they donate it to a youth center in town, a refuge that helped them both before they came to live with me.

I work a six-hour shift at Arcania, picking produce, before heading home and doing it all over again the next day. I've grown closer to Spencer than I could've possibly imagined and while nothing has happened between us yet, I know it's only a matter of time.

Until Cora arrives.

I'm sorting apples when Harlan's convertible screeches to a stop outside the main house and *she* gets out, all wide-eyed innocence. She's slim, blonde, pretty, and when I see Spencer almost fall over his feet in a rush to take her on a tour, I know she's trouble.

Spencer introduces us, but Cora barely acknowledges I exist. That's okay, because being in the background means I can watch her—and make sure she stays away from my man.

But as every day passes, I realize Spencer isn't mine. Sure, he's still friendly toward me and we share our usual jokes and banter, but his eyes are only on Cora. He's an idiot, because it's clear Harlan has dibs on her, but that doesn't stop Spencer. He moons after her like a love-struck fool and my resentment festers.

Mel and Freda notice something's wrong, but I don't confide in them. They're already a hundred times more worldly than I am and articulating how I've had a crush for weeks and haven't done anything about it only makes me look like an idiot.

So I bide my time. Surely Cora's newness will wear off soon enough and Spencer will grow tired of her?

Harlan's definitely courting her, which is strange considering she's a runaway according to Spencer and an employee. But I see the way Harlan looks at her, like she's his possession, and while his obsessiveness is a tad creepy, I'm glad. There's no way in hell Spencer will cross Harlan.

Cora has been at Arcania for a month when we're thrust together to pick strawberries. She's barely said two words to me in the previous four weeks, so I'm surprised when she starts up a conversation.

"How come you don't live here?"

"I share a place with some friends." I must tread carefully because I don't want her tattling to Spencer. He thinks I live with a few roommates—which is technically true—

but Cora has this way of looking at me like she sees straight through me.

"Lucky you." She jerks a thumb over her shoulder. "I know I'm lucky to have room and board here, but living in the mansion gives me the creeps."

I know the feeling. While Mel and Freda haven't said anything, I swear I hear footsteps walking the hallways at night at home. Ever since I hung that sign up, The Haven has come to life. Slamming doors, flickering lights, even giggling once when I was home alone. I figure the ghosts are friendly. Maybe those witches Mel mentioned making themselves known. I could take the sign down, but that would invite more questions from the girls and it's easier to leave it up.

"It's definitely got a gothic vibe," I say, plucking strawberries at a furious pace so I don't have to spend too long with her.

She glances at my fast-moving fingers and raises a brow. "They don't pay bonuses, you know."

I force a chuckle. "I enjoy working fast. Makes the day go quicker."

She stares at me like I'm mad, so I divert her attention by fishing for information.

"Do you have a boyfriend?"

She hesitates and glances around before responding. "No. But Harlan's persistent and he's handsome and..."

I hope she won't say 'and I really like Spencer instead,' but I prompt her. "And?"

"And I'm a tad nervous that if I rebuff him, I'll get fired."

I glimpse fear in her eyes and in that moment, I feel sorry for her. Harlan gives off bad vibes and I pity her for drawing his attention.

"That wouldn't be fair."

She snickers. "Since when is life fair?"

"Good point."

"What are you, eighteen?"

When I nod, she continues. "Considering you're working here and you live with roommates, I'm guessing your home life wasn't great either."

"Yeah, so?"

"So you understand that we have limited options and fairness rarely comes into it."

Guilt gnaws at me. Courtesy of my trust fund, I have many options. And the fact Cora is fearful of rejecting Harlan because it may affect her employment status reinforces how lucky I am not to be dependent on the whims of others.

"Don't let Harlan push you into anything you're not ready for," I say, sounding like a lecturing parent and expecting her to scoff.

But Cora nods again, her expression pensive. "I do like him. And a small part of me can't help but think how much easier my life would be if we got together."

I refrain from warning her that Harlan's idea of them 'getting together' and hers might be worlds apart. Rich guys like Harlan rarely date poor girls like Cora. They use and discard them. But she's old enough to take care of herself and as long as she's mulling over Harlan, she'll leave Spencer alone. I hope.

"What do you think of Spencer?"

I stiffen but force my fingers to keep plucking strawberries. "He's nice."

"Yeah, he is." Her soft sigh is almost imperceptible, but I hear it and warning bells clang in my head. "Life is complicated sometimes."

I'm about to ask what she means when Harlan appears

out of nowhere. He barely glances my way before his intense stare settles on Cora.

"I want to show you something," he says, his silky-smooth tone making me want to take a bath.

Cora's expression is resigned as she stands and swipes her hands down the side of her jeans. "Will it take long? Leah and I must finish picking these before sundown."

The wave of his hand is dismissive. "I'm sure Leah can finish up."

He doesn't even look at me and I'm relieved. No way do I want to be on his radar. From his carefully combed hair to the soles of his designer loafers, Harlan radiates slime. I should know. He's exactly the kind of guy Mom and Dad tried to foist on me as 'suitable dating material.' Sons of their cronies, spoiled rich boys who had no boundaries because even if they slipped up they knew their parents would pay to get them out of trouble.

I know this is why I chose Chad to lose my virginity to. He was the exact opposite of the clean-cut clones my folks favored. Chad had shoulder-length black hair, played bass guitar in a garage band, and spray-painted stunning graffiti murals when he wasn't slacking off at school. He was a scholarship kid at the exclusive private school I attended, and he was everything I wanted to be: rebellious, confident, comfortable in his own skin.

He never would've made a good father, which is why I had no intention of telling him about the baby. Unfair, maybe, but irrelevant now, thanks to my controlling folks.

Lost in my musings, I startle when Cora taps me on the shoulder. "Are you okay with finishing this job?"

"Absolutely." I make a little shooing motion with my hands and I pity her again when her expression is crestfallen, like she'd been hoping I'd stand up to Harlan and demand she help me finish picking the strawberries.

Harlan stands too close to her as they walk away, his hand deliberately grazing hers, and I suppress a shudder. They're almost out of sight when I see Spencer watching their retreating backs too, and his expression is wistful.

SEVENTEEN

RYLEE

NOW

An hour after I re-read Mom's first letter for the umpteenth time, I hear my grandmother's car pull out of the drive. Good. I need to speak to Dad. Alone.

He's in the kitchen, sitting at the small round table in the corner where we share our meals. At any given time, there's between two and twenty people staying at The Haven, but Gran insisted we keep dinners private, just the three of us.

Growing up, I liked meeting the various runaways who drifted through our house. It made me feel like I had a lot of friends, when in reality I had none. Even when I hit my teens, when most kids are making connections online, I could only use the computer for schoolwork, and social media was forbidden. It made me a freak. Then again, who knew? Apart from my teachers online and the inhabitants of The Haven who drifted in and out of my life, I had zero contact with the outside world, and I couldn't miss what I'd never really had.

I could've danced for joy when I recently got a cell, even if I'm sure Gran monitors my calls. That's the thing about depending financially on someone. Everything we buy is via credit cards, either online or in person, so Gran sees the records. What's crazier, she convinced Dad when he first arrived here that having access to a cell might trigger the memories he'd deliberately suppressed so he doesn't have one. We're definitely a family of freaks and it hasn't really bothered me.

Until now.

Reading Mom's letter has changed everything and has me questioning my grandmother's motivations big time.

"Hey Lee, have you been reading in your room?" Dad looks up from the partially completed jigsaw on the table. "There's some quiche you can heat if you're hungry."

"I'm good, thanks." I sit opposite him and pick up a piece of the puzzle that belongs near the top left corner and press it into place. "Where's Gran?"

"Had an errand to run in Nag's Head so she'll be gone awhile."

To get to Nag's Head, Gran has to drive through Flotilla Firth, and my newly awakened suspicions make me wonder if she's visiting Arcania despite her protestations she didn't know the place.

"That was weird about Maisey saying Gran used to work at Arcania, huh?"

My father's fingers convulse, dislodging the puzzle pieces he's carefully arranged in the lower corner and sending them scattering to the floor. He's pale, his eyes wide, almost catatonic.

"Dad, are you okay?"

Fear makes bile rise in my throat as he continues to stare at me, unseeing, and I'm torn between hugging him or getting him a glass of water. "Dad?"

I stand and move around to his side of the table, and when I lay a comforting hand on his shoulder he flinches. But the movement brings him back to the present as he stands and rushes over to the sink. For a moment I think he's going to vomit, but he turns on the tap and ducks his head down to guzzle water like he's parched in the desert.

I don't get it. I'd mentioned Arcania before, when I asked him about it in front of Gran. I replay the earlier scene in my head, belatedly realizing that's not quite true. Before, I'd mentioned Gran working at a wellness center, but hadn't specifically said the name.

What is it about Arcania that triggered my father?

When he's drunk his fill, he turns off the tap and swipes his mouth with his sleeve. Some of his color has returned, but his skin still has a greenish tinge.

"Sorry about that, kiddo. Not sure what came over me." His smile is wan as he rejoins me at the table and gives me a swift hug before pointing at the puzzle. "Want to help me finish this?"

I want answers, but I can't push Dad, not after what I just witnessed.

I shake my head. "You go ahead. I think I'll take a walk."

"Okay, see you later."

I'm unsure whether to leave him, but as he resumes pondering the puzzle, he appears perfectly normal, and I'll gain nothing from staying.

One thing for certain is, this is the first time I can

remember that my father has had a physical reaction like that to anything, and it revolves around Arcania.

What is it about that place that has mysterious ties to my grandmother, and now my father?

Only one way to find out.

I need to pay Arcania a visit.

EIGHTEEN

LEAH

THEN

Over the next week, Spencer withdraws. He's sullen rather than his usual cheery self, and I know the cause.

Cora and Harlan.

Daphne, who works in the kitchen, told me that Harlan's been courting Cora every night, down at some cove on the beach. The rumor mill is rife, but nobody dares say anything for fear of incurring Harlan's wrath and losing their job.

For what it's worth, Cora doesn't look like a woman in love. She seems stoic and I silently cheer that if Harlan's persistence pays off, soon Spencer will be all mine.

I'm clocking off Friday evening—I pulled a double shift because a worker had food poisoning—when there's a tap on my shoulder.

I whirl around to find Spencer smiling at me; the first time I've seen him smile all week. "Hey, how are you?"

"Better now it's the end of a long week. Are you doing anything tonight?"

Saying I'm heading home to order a pizza and watch sitcom reruns with Mel and Freda sounds lame, but before I can answer he says, "Because the workers are having a party in the orchard, if you want to come?"

"Sure, sounds good," I say, without hesitation. Spencer inviting me to a party is a sign he's over Cora.

"I'll meet you over there." He leans in close and for an irrational second I think he's going to kiss me. "Word of warning. Stay clear of the punch. A few of the older guys are into hallucinogens and spike it at random times."

I'm already giddy enough at the prospect of spending an evening with Spencer. The last thing I need is drugs.

"Thanks for letting me know."

Emboldened by his invitation, I touch his arm. If he experiences the same zap I do he doesn't show it, and with a smile he's gone, headed toward the house.

Maybe Spencer is oblivious to my crush and tonight is the night to change that? There's a feeling in the air, anticipation mixed with excitement, and as a country song heavy on guitar starts up, I follow the music to the orchard.

The smell of ripe apples is redolent as I weave between the trees to the clearing in the middle, where a trestle has been set up. It's draped in a filmy white chiffon and loaded with large plates of bruschetta and a charcuterie board. I steer clear of the punch bowl perched on the end and snag a soda instead.

Daphne spots me and waves me over. "Is this your first orchard twilight party?"

I nod. "Uh-huh. Spencer invited me."

"Well, you're welcome anytime. All the workers are."

"Thanks." I barely know the other employees because once we clock on, we work hard. Magnus, an intimidating mountain of a man who scares me more than Harlan, and Helga make regular rounds of the orchard, checking up on us.

"Have they tried to rope you into getting a tattoo yet?"

Tattoo? Me? Not likely. My fear of needles is entrenched, and nobody is getting near me with ink.

"By they, do you mean the other workers?"

She shakes her head. "The Medville's. I'm guessing you're too new, but eventually they like everyone who works and lives here to get the tattoo."

I don't live here, so I'm hoping that counts me out. "Do you have one?"

She nods, slips off her sandal, and lifts her foot. "Here. Look. Everyone gets it on their heel."

A strange compass that's Arcania's emblem is tattooed on the sole of her left heel in vivid turquoise ink. "It's pretty."

"Hurt like the devil." She lowers her foot and slips her sandal back on. "Do you know much about the history behind the *vegvisir*?"

I don't and I'm interested to hear what Daphne has to say until I spy something that makes my heart clench.

While I've been studying Daphne's tattoo, Spencer and Cora have arrived. She empties her cup of punch in three gulps, then follows him into the shadows of the trees.

I'm desperate to follow, but I'm terrified of what I may see.

CHAPTER
NINETEEN

RYLEE

NOW

I don't go for a walk after Dad's weird reaction to me mentioning Arcania. Instead, I go to my room and start reading Mom's second letter to me.

Dear Rylee,

Happy first birthday, sweetheart! You're growing into such a gorgeous girl. Freda sent me a photo she took at your birthday party and you're adorable. She also sends me regular updates via text whenever she sees you, and I'm so relieved to hear your grandmother is doting and isn't inflicting her special brand of crazy on you. Sounds like her possessiveness is the reason she threatened and banished me and that she's actually capable of love.

Because that's my greatest wish, Rylee, that you're raised in a loving home. Freda said she's protective of you also and that your father has stepped up. Not that I expected anything less. John is a sweet guy and I miss him.

I've settled in Miami and I'm working as a personal assistant to a gym manager. It's not glamorous but my boss is nice, the job is easy, and I'm saving every cent I can. My dream is to get a small house where we can live when you're old enough to make your own decisions and hopefully, want to be with me.

I know it's going to be a lot to ask when you're over eighteen and have thought I abandoned you, but I'm hoping that you'll give me a chance, sweet girl. Because being your mom is everything to me.

I love you.

Mom xx

I DON'T CRY after reading this one. Maybe because I shed enough tears to fill the Atlantic after reading the first a hundred times, but I feel closer to Mom letting her words lull me, convince me, that she's not some evil person who walked away from her baby without looking back.

I need to see Freda, but I'm not sure how much more she can tell me, other than she sent Mom updates over the years. Visiting Arcania is my priority, and that's where I'm headed tomorrow. I'll have to time my departure for when Gran's busy because no way will she buy an excuse I have to head into town again. I rarely go into Edgewater Bay unless she sends me on an errand.

But first, I have to get through dinner. I take a nap after reading the letter and only wake when there's a light knock on my door.

"Sweetie, it's time for dinner," Dad says, and I'm glad he sounds normal after his freak out a few hours ago.

"Be there in a sec," I call out, knuckling the sleep from

my eyes and hoping that with a little luck, Gran will still be out. She has an uncanny knack of picking up on any off vibes and after the day I've had—especially the doubts raised by my mom's letters and Dad's reaction to my mention of Arcania—the last thing I need is her pinning me with one of her famous stares or worse, interrogating me.

However, when I enter the kitchen, Gran's back and I paste a smile on my face as I transfer the bowl of salad from the counter to the dining table.

"Did you nap, Rylee?" Gran asks, her gaze sweeping over my face. "That's not like you."

I shrug, feigning nonchalance. "I was tired and thought it couldn't hurt."

"Naps are restorative," Dad chimes in, his smile soft as our eyes meet. "Maybe I should've had one after what happened earlier."

I stiffen and Gran's laser-like stare zeroes in on him. "What happened earlier?"

My father belatedly realizes his mistake, because I've seen Gran's obsession with his health, particularly his memory, over the years, and if it bothers me, he must be over it.

"Nothing, really. I must've stood too quickly and felt faint. Rylee got me some water to drink, so all good."

Dad can't meet my eyes, so either he's lying, or he genuinely doesn't know why he had a mini-meltdown at the mention of Arcania.

Gran's not buying it and her narrow-eyed glare focuses on me. "Is that right?"

I nod. "Yeah, we've all done it, standing too quickly and feeling woozy. I made him sit down afterward and have some water."

"Plus, I ate two quiches, so that helped." Dad pats his stomach and grins. "Must've been low blood sugar."

We all know Dad has a bottomless stomach and can eat all day yet still be hungry, so his self-deprecation defuses the situation.

However, throughout dinner Gran watches Dad to the point he excuses himself on the pretext of catching up on an ocean documentary he missed last night, and flees. I don't blame him. Being a witness to that intense scrutiny is disconcerting. How much worse must it be for Dad?

As soon as he leaves the kitchen, Gran turns to me. "Now tell me what really happened."

Oh boy.

"We told you."

"And I don't believe you."

"Are you calling me a liar, Gran? Because that's totally uncalled for."

"I've always had a good radar for reading people and there's something wrong with your father. It worries me."

I want to tell her to back off, that he's fine. But a small part of me wants to sow a seed of doubt and see how she reacts.

"Maybe he's recovering his memories?"

Gran flushes an angry puce. "What makes you say that?"

"He got this funny glazed look in his eyes before he almost fainted, so I thought maybe he'd remembered something from his past?"

"Did he say that?" She practically yells, and I guess I have my answer about why she's overprotective with Dad.

She's worried he'll get his memory back and not need her anymore. Ludicrous, because he'll always care about

Gran. She's his only family, apart from me, but from her reaction, she's seriously freaked.

It reiterates what Mom said in her first letter, that Gran was extremely possessive of Dad. I can understand why she wouldn't want him to remember potential trauma from his past because it might dredge up a host of unwelcome pain, but he's a grown man and not the young guy barely out of his teens when he first arrived here.

"No, Gran, he hasn't said he remembered anything. I was just surmising out loud."

"Don't," she snaps, her glower formidable. "Your father's suffering from dissociative amnesia for a reason, which means his past is too painful to recall. He has remembered nothing in two decades and I hope, for his sake, he doesn't start now."

My nod is meek, but all I can think is, *for his sake or yours.*

TWENTY

LEAH

THEN

C ora and Spencer don't reappear for thirty minutes.

I'm torn between going in search of them and drowning my sorrows in spiked punch. But then I'll be too drunk to drive and the last thing I need is a DUI. Not to mention I'll be forced to spend the night here and see the aftermath of whatever Cora and Spencer have been up to.

It doesn't take an Einstein to figure it out and the thought of the two of them together makes my stomach churn. Nausea makes me woozy, and I lurch away from the orchard, the pungent aromas of roasting chickens and marijuana not helping. I'm almost at my car when Harlan's convertible pulls into the car park area beside the mansion. He always drives too fast and I scowl as a spray of gravel peppers me.

He kills the engine and vaults over the door, and to my surprise, he makes a beeline for me. "Hey, sorry about that. Are you okay?"

"I'll live."

Either he doesn't see my glower in the darkness or chooses to ignore it because he's the high and mighty Harlan Medville. "Why don't you live onsite like the rest of the workers?"

So much for his concern.

"Because I have a house I like."

My droll response makes the corners of his mouth twitch with amusement. "So that means you don't like Arcania?"

"I like working here just fine."

"Good, because we value our employees." He takes a step closer and in that moment, I realize how alone we are. The music from the orchard is loud, so even if he tried something and I scream, no-one will hear me. "It's Leah, yeah?"

I nod and surreptitiously slide my hand into my pocket, comforted when I grasp my keys. A good weapon if I need it, though stabbing the boss will no doubt get me fired. Not that I'll care if he puts a hand on me. Harlan makes my skin crawl. He's smarmy and smug and Cora deserves him. I assume the attraction is his money, but I wouldn't let him near me, no matter how starving or how broke I was.

"Have you been diving yet, Leah?"

"No."

Maybe if I keep my answers brief, he'll leave me alone?

No such luck, as he closes the distance between us even more. "That's a shame. Perhaps I can teach you?"

He's going to touch me, I can feel it. Every hair on my body stands on end, and I grip my keys tighter.

"I'm not a fan of the water. Why don't you give Cora lessons?"

Flinging his girlfriend's name in his face does the trick. He pauses and glances over my shoulder. "Have you seen her?"

I have two choices. Throw Cora under the bus like I want to or save Spencer. Because I know without a doubt if I tell Harlan where they are and he finds them together, Spencer will get fired and I'll lose the first guy I've ever loved before we've had a chance to see if we can build a relationship.

It's foolish to harbor hope, considering he's probably having sex with Cora right now, but maybe I'm wrong and they're just taking a walk? So if I send Harlan in their direction and I've made a mistake, I can ruin both their jobs. I'm not a vindictive person, no matter how much envy is eating away at me.

Besides, I care about Spencer and can't risk hurting him, so I say, "I think I saw her go for a walk with a few of the girls a while ago."

"Okay, thanks." He steps back, and I breathe a sigh of relief. But his eyes are still predatory, and my skin feels like I've taken a bath in slime. "If you ever need anything, Leah, come find me."

I force a smile, when in reality I feel like puking. "Sure."

Thankfully, he steps aside so I can get into my car, but my hands shake as I fumble with the keys. I have no idea how Cora can stand being near Harlan, let alone have him touch her. Though I'm not a complete idiot. I've seen young women paraded around as rich guys' girlfriends all the time in my parents' world. Money talks, especially if you're desperate enough, and it's not my place to judge Cora. As long as she's not toying with Spencer.

I've never been so relieved to leave Arcania behind and as I glance in my rear vision mirror as I drive away, Harlan is watching me.

TWENTY-ONE

RYLEE

NOW

After Gran's weirdness at dinner, I need comforting, and despite my intentions to ration out Mom's letters, I can't help but pull out the third one.

DEAR RYLEE,

I can't believe my baby girl is two! Happy birthday, sweetheart. I wish I could be there in person to give you a big cuddle, but know I'm always thinking of you, every minute of the day and night.

I've started a tradition. Every year I write this letter just before your birthday, I buy a charm. I bought the bracelet not long after I left you, because I saw it in a jewelry shop window, a shop called Riley's, and it reminded me of you. My plan is to give it to you if you find me after your eighteenth birthday, so you'll have eighteen charms as a reminder that I never forgot you.

I hope my letters aren't too upsetting for you because that's not my intention. I want you to feel closer to me, not alienate you further. The thought of you hating me for leaving you...it's haunted me every day since I walked away. My heart has always been with you, no matter how far away I am. I'm so tempted to move closer to you, on the off chance I'll be able to see you even at a distance. But I don't trust Leah. She has the funds and the reach to annihilate me if she wants to. And if you're as wise as I think you are (I mean, you've got this far, going in search of me and discovering these letters via Barry Mackay) I hope you realize she's not to be trusted too.

I hate that every letter sounds like I'm trying to poison your mind and turn you against her, but I'm not, truly. I'm merely a scared mother who'll do anything to protect her child.

On a happier note, I'm still loving my job and I'm saving for a deposit on a small house I've seen. It's been on the market for ten months, so I'm hoping the realtor will give it away at a bargain price when I make an offer in a few weeks. It's the cutest cottage close to the beach. Two bedrooms, a large bay window in the living room, and a reading nook.

Freda tells me you love books and that even at two, your ability to decipher words is incredible. I'm so proud of you, sweetheart. And it makes my heart joyful to think we might one day cuddle up in that reading nook and trade opinions on our favorite books.

I can't wait for that day.

Until next year, gorgeous girl...

Love you,

Mom xx

MY EYES ARE damp when I finish the letter and I carefully refold it, slide it back in the envelope, and add it to the stack but at the bottom. I position the box in its hidden hole and maneuver the floorboard over it. Only then do I climb onto my bed, lie down, and close my eyes.

It should make me feel better Mom shares my doubts about Gran's trustworthiness, but it doesn't. Instead, I feel like the biggest fool in the world for not being more aware sooner.

How much is Gran hiding?

And how far will she go to protect Dad and me?

TWENTY-TWO

LEAH

THEN

When I get home, all I want is to take a long soak in a hot tub. Having that sleaze Harlan pay me attention makes me want to scrub my skin, hard.

I don't like that I'm on his radar now. Men like that wield their power relentlessly, and if they see something or someone as a challenge...I shudder and rub my bare arms. Definitely time for that bath.

However, as I enter the house, the lights go out. More precisely, the living room lights, and I hear a giggle, followed by a shush. I smile, the sounds of my housemates the exact welcome home I need. When I'd left Harrisburg I wanted to be alone, but after living with Mel and Freda, I realize that when I fled my past it's my parents I didn't want to live with, and the girls are a nice reprieve.

They've mentioned a few others looking for a place to stay and the thought of filling The Haven with those who need sanctuary makes me feel good in a way I never anticipated when I first invited Mel to stay. Too many teens are homeless and if I can use my money to help alleviate the problems of even a few, it's well spent.

I've contemplated asking Cora if she wants to stay here. I know she's a runaway, and that's how she ended up at Arcania. But we're not close and the last thing I need is for her to tell Harlan she's moving out and to where. This place may be The Haven in name, but that's exactly what it is for me. A place away from everything. Untainted. And I want it to stay that way.

When I reach the living room, I see the girls carefully sliding a navy glass bowl out of a black silk cloth.

"What are you doing?" I ask, and they jump, their heads snapping up in unison.

"Damn it, Leah, you almost made me drop it," Mel mutters, clutching the bowl to her chest. "Stop creeping around."

"I would've assumed you heard my car pull up." I point to the bowl. "What are you hiding, and why are you in the dark?"

"It's a scrying bowl, and we're about to take it outside," Freda says, her expression solemn. "We've been planning this for a month."

I've gotten used to the house's oddities—the floorboards creaking at night like someone's tiptoeing around, the occasional slamming door, the flickering lights—but a shiver of foreboding makes me fold my arms around my middle. "Planning what?"

"Preparing the scrying bowl so we can get answers from the spirit world." Mel's tone is as serious as Freda's expression. "We think that if we talk to the witches who used to live here, they might leave us alone."

I don't want to encourage them, but I'm not stupid. If I dismiss this as a ridiculous waste of time, they'll clam up and won't tell me what they mean by 'leave us alone.'

"Have the witches been bothering you?" There's a question I never thought I'd ask.

Freda's gaze darts around the room before she responds. "It's just a feeling we both get. Like we're being watched all the time."

"And we want it to stop," Mel adds, biting her bottom lip.

I can see they're seriously spooked and if whatever ritual they've concocted will placate them, I'll go along with it. "Okay. So what do we do?"

Mel and Freda exchange glances, before Mel says, "You want to help us?"

"Sure. I hear things in the house too, but it's not malevolent, so I don't worry so much."

"We're not worried." Freda squares her shoulders, but I see beneath her false bravado when her fingers bunch the black silk bag. "But if you want to help, I guess that's okay."

Mel gives a brief nod. "We need to do this outside, in the full moon."

I follow them outside and refrain from rolling my eyes as they place the bowl on a table, fill it with water, and add a few drops of black ink to it.

"We've already prepped the bowl last month, by making an infusion of mugwort, which has been used by witches for centuries to promote second sight, rubbing the inside of the bowl with it, then letting it sit all night to absorb the moon's powers." Freda glances up at the sky, her eyes wide. "Then it had to be wrapped in a black silk cloth and kept in a dark cupboard for a month, until the next full moon, which is tonight."

Mel nods. "Now we stare at the moon's reflection in the water, wave our hand over the surface three times, and ask it to show us what we want to know."

I bite back my first retort, 'that must be some powerful water in a bowl.'

"If you focus hard enough and try to see beyond the moon's reflection in the bowl, images or symbols might appear," Freda says. "I'm hoping if the witches show up, we'll get to know they're friendly."

"And don't worry, we'll smudge everything when we're finished to banish any ghosts," Mel says.

As my parents used to say, the Internet is a problem because it feeds people's obsessions and I'm beginning to think they're right. These two girls have looked up some weird spells and honestly think they're going to connect with witches from the past.

But I've just been thinking about how much I enjoy having them as housemates. The last thing I need is to scare them off by belittling their choices.

"So all I have to do is stare at the moon's reflection in the water?"

They nod in unison. "Yep."

"Okay then," I murmur, trying not to laugh as they whisper some weird incantation about inky blackness and the moon's secret power, while their hands drift over the water's surface in a circular motion.

We stare at the water in silence, the surface barely rippling despite a sudden breeze. I see nothing but the moon for several minutes and just when I'm about to say I'm done, I hear Freda gasp, and Mel's sharp intake of breath a second later.

A slight swirl in the water has me leaning forward, and that's when I see it.

A baby's bassinet.

With a blue sign pinned to it and Baby Smith in swirling calligraphy.

My heart stops and I break into a cold sweat.

I blink. Once. Twice. Refocus.

The baby is now a young man, floating in the ocean, pale and lifeless.

Then he opens his eyes and stares straight at me.

TWENTY-THREE

RYLEE

NOW

M y plans to visit Arcania today are thwarted when Dad corners me in the garden after breakfast.

"Lee, I've got something to tell you."

Dad's pale and his eyes are darting everywhere, and my heart sinks that maybe he's about to have another episode like he did yesterday when I mentioned Arcania. If so, it's my fault.

"Are you okay, Dad?" I lean into him, resting my head on his shoulder. "You don't look so good."

"I'm fine, but this is big." His arm slides around my waist and hugs me tight for a moment before releasing me. "I remembered something." His lips thin. "From my past."

As if I need the clarification. For so long I've wondered what my father went through to obliterate his memories completely. I've been equal parts curious and terrified because I don't want him to spiral if his memories come back and they're horrific, but I also want to know more about where we came from and if we have extended family. Now it's happened, and he appears relatively unscathed and wants to talk about it, I'm ready to listen.

Dad recovering his first memory in decades is big. So huge that my first instinct is to run to Gran, but then I remember all the reasons why I shouldn't, and I clamp down on the urge.

Besides, the fact my father has come to me about this and not Gran speaks volumes. Unless he's already told her? Doubtful, considering she wouldn't have let him out of her sight if he had.

"Have you told Gran?"

He shakes his head, a small frown creasing his brow. "You know what she's like. The way she overreacted at dinner last night when she learned I'd had a bit of a turn... no, it's better she doesn't know."

"I agree."

He pinches the bridge of his nose, but Dad doesn't look stressed. "I've been petrified of remembering my past since I turned up at The Haven. The doc said don't push it and your Gran agreed. We eschewed seeing a therapist because of it. I wanted to leave well enough alone, you know?"

He gives a little shake of his head. "Yesterday, I don't know what happened when you mentioned Arcania. I have no recognition of the name, but maybe it jolted something in my brain because I woke up in the middle of the night and remembered a woman."

My hearts pounding and I lean forward to grasp his hand. I give a gentle squeeze of encouragement.

"There was nothing remotely bad about the memory. In

fact, all I felt was warmth and happiness." He blinks several times, the slight glaze in his eyes implying he's lost in recollection. "We were holding hands and walking on a beach. She loved me because I heard her say it. It felt...right."

Dad's serene expression gives me hope that it'll be okay if I ask probing questions.

"Did you recognize the beach? Is it near here?"

He shakes his head. "I don't know it. It wasn't any of the beaches along this stretch of the Outer Banks."

"And the woman? It wasn't Mom?"

"No, sweetheart, it wasn't." He turns his palm over and threads his fingers through mine. "This was a memory preceding my time here. I know because I didn't recognize the place or woman, when I remember every tiny detail about your mom."

He taps his head with his free hand. "I fell for her quickly, and not a day goes by I don't wonder where she went and if she's okay."

Guilt makes heat creep into my cheeks. I could set his mind at ease, tell him about the letters. But I want to finish them first and see if Mom's okay with me divulging the truth to him. It's the least I can do.

"Do you think you should see a therapist? See if you can recover more memories?"

He grimaces. "To be honest, I'm not sure. Just because I remember one pleasant memory, doesn't mean the rest will be. All the research I've done is clear on that. Whatever happened to me, it's bad enough to make my brain effectively wipe out the horror, and I'm reluctant to dredge up all that now, after so long."

"I get it." And I do, but a part of me wishes I could rattle free every suppressed memory so I know more about where we came from. "Have you ever thought about trying to trace your biological family?"

His eyebrows rise. "Via one of those online family history sites, you mean?"

"Yeah."

"I have thought about it, but what would be the point? I wouldn't recognize any of the names if they pop up, and what if one of the people I reconnect with turns out to be the psycho I fled from?"

"Good point." I chew on the inside of my cheek and Dad must sense my hesitancy, because he says, "You're curious, aren't you? About how I got here?"

I nod. "Don't get me wrong, Dad, you've been an incredible parent and I love you, but a part of me wants to know more about our family."

"I understand." He tips my chin up to look into my eyes. "I know you, sweetheart, and if you're contemplating doing one of those DNA tests online, be careful, okay? If whoever put me through a trauma big enough to wipe my memory is out there trying to find me, I don't want you getting mixed up in it." His expression is somber. "It could be dangerous, and I don't want to tempt fate."

I hadn't thought about doing a DNA test in years, not since middle school biology, when the thought popped into my head while we were studying genes. But hearing Dad mention it...it's a great idea. It might reveal more about Mom's family, too.

"You're going to do it, aren't you?"

"You know me too well." I smile and rest my head against Dad's shoulder. "It'll be okay. We'll keep this between us, and I'll let you know what I discover, okay?"

"Okay." He presses a kiss on the top of my head, like he

used to when I was little and would skin my knees from overzealous running. "Love you, kiddo."

"Love you too, Dad."

I just hope my curiosity about our family isn't going to upend our well-ordered world.

TWENTY-FOUR

LEAH

THEN

Mel and Freda declare the psychic scrying bowl a success. Mel saw a hooded figure opening its arms to her in a hug, Freda saw a smiling witch, so they think the witches of days gone by inhabiting The Haven are friendly. I could've told them that without the scrying because nothing bad has happened in the house. What's a few creaks and groans between ancient friends?

Me, on the other hand, have more questions than answers after that bizarre ritual I don't believe in. I go through the motions of smudging with the girls, waving smoldering sage over each other like a cleansing cosmic shower, then waving it in every nook of the house, banishing any potential evil.

Unfortunately for me, the only evil in my life is my parents, and I thought I'd banished them when I left. But seeing that baby, clearly a boy by the name tag color, in a bassinet marked Baby Smith, has me wondering exactly how depraved they are.

Did they lie to me about my baby dying?

It makes little sense, considering my baby was being adopted out regardless. They wouldn't even tell me the sex, deeming it irrelevant and potential hurtful if I knew. Ha. Like knowing whether I had a boy or girl would dim the excruciating agony I'd gone through at having my choice to raise a child ripped away from me. Then to be told I wouldn't bear any more kids...

They had no reason to lie about my baby dying, but what if they had? Are they that narcissistic that they feared I'd go searching for my biological child one day and they couldn't bear the stigma even years later?

I'd put nothing past them, but I'm basing all this supposition on a weird ritual I don't believe in. Beyond foolish. I can't explain why those images appeared to me and the girls saw something entirely different. Heck, I can't explain why I saw anything reflected in that murky water. And maybe I don't want to.

Besides, I have more important things to worry about. When I return to work the next morning, Spencer has completely withdrawn. He doesn't tease me like he usually does. He barely acknowledges I exist, which makes me fear the worst.

He had sex with Cora last night, just as I suspected when they disappeared together.

I don't treat him any differently, but my heart breaks over the next week as we work alongside each other and our conversation is stilted rather than free flowing. Interestingly, Cora avoids Spencer and the few times I see her, she's fawning over Harlan.

I can't fathom it. If she's been intimate with Spencer and they like each other, why is she wasting time on slimy Harlan? Sure, she might be fearful of losing her job, but if she really cares about Spencer, the simple solution would be for them to leave Arcania and start their relationship elsewhere.

The thought makes my stomach cramp and I press my hand to it. I'm supposed to have a crush on Spencer, nothing more, but the churning in my gut at the thought of him leaving means I have deeper feelings.

"Hey, are you okay?"

Great, just what I need, the guy I think I've foolishly fallen in love with checking up on me.

I force a smile that must come out a grimace, considering his raised eyebrow. "Yeah. Skipped breakfast."

"Want me to grab you something from the kitchen? I think Daph has leftover scrambled egg burritos from this morning."

His concern is touching if I thought he really cared. But I know differently. He prefers Cora to me, and my stomach somersaults again.

"Thanks, but I'm okay. I'll have an extra helping at lunch."

I've never been any good at hiding my feelings—which is why my mom figured out my pregnancy before I was ready to tell her—and my response is terse.

A frown dents Spencer's brow. "Did I do something to annoy you?"

Here's my chance to tell him how I feel. How I think he's making a big mistake in falling for Cora. How I'd love him to be my first official boyfriend.

Instead, I settle for a semi-truth. "You invited me to the employee party last week, then disappeared. Not cool."

He flinches like I've struck him. "But you know everyone else. I didn't think you expected me to hang around all night."

"I don't expect anything from you," I snap, failing to clamp down on my anger. "But just so you know, some of the other workers may not be as discreet as me and if they gossip to Harlan about you and Cora, you'll both probably get fired."

He blanches, leaving his eyes stark against the pallor. "What do you mean?"

"I'm not an idiot, Spencer. I saw the two of you disappear in the orchard. What were you doing, picking apples?"

My sarcasm strikes a chord as his jaw clenches. "My relationship with Cora is none of your business, or anybody else's for that matter."

I snort. "You don't get it. Harlan has dibs on her so you don't have a relationship with Cora, and if you do, you're an idiot, because..." I trail off, my heart breaking because he's obtuse and completely oblivious to my feelings, but not wanting to hurt him at the same time.

"Because what?"

I sigh. There's no easy way to say this. "Because if it comes to a decision between the two of you, she'll choose him every time."

His eyes narrow as he takes a step back. "I never picked you to be spiteful." A sneer curls his upper lip. "What are you, jealous?"

"What if I am?"

I fling it out there, the closest I'll come to a declaration of how I feel.

Sadly, he's shocked, which means he's never contemplated the two of us in a relationship, and our playfulness this entire time has been purely based on friendship.

Before he can say anything, Cora appears.

"Hey, you two. I've got news." She claps her hands like an excited kid, her smile wide and clueless. "I'm getting married."

I should be elated, but as I see the devastation creep into Spencer's eyes, I know I'll never mean as much to him as Cora does.

TWENTY-FIVE

RYLEE

NOW

Gran has me doing so many chores for the next few days that I don't have time to follow up on my plans: head into town to the library to research genealogy sites and visit Arcania. We have four new residents arriving at The Haven, referred from a local women's shelter, so we have time to prepare, not like some of our usual walk-ins.

We air out rooms, change linen, dust every surface, stock the closets and bathrooms, and put fresh flowers everywhere. Gran likes to welcome every person who arrives on our doorstep with a care package too, and I've always loved helping her make them. Cute little wicker baskets we fill with cookies, bath bombs, body lotion, vouchers for online books, fluffy socks, chocolate truffles, and handmade soaps.

Her generosity is one of the things I love about her.

She's selfless, treating every person who comes through The Haven's doors as family. Not that everyone passing through has been grateful. We've had a few who are angry at the world and all in it—probably for good reason considering the fraught situations some have fled—but Gran doesn't tolerate BS either and those who disrupt the serenity here are encouraged to leave.

"Rylee, have you seen the new lavender scented candles I ordered?" Gran opens the linen closet where she stocks stuff for the care packages. "They're perfect for our new guests."

Gran's a firm believer in aromatherapy and I know she wants the lavender to help the battered women relax. We've had many referrals from the shelter over the years and Gran treats them all with extra kindness. Most are skittish, scared, even resentful, but Gran has this way about her that makes everyone feel welcome. I particularly remember a guy who'd been physically abused by his wife for a number of years and she'd been so gentle with him I often had to leave the room for fear they'd see the tears in my eyes.

"Sorry, haven't seen them," I say, hating that I'm lying to the woman I've just been thinking about in such glowing terms.

I know exactly where the candles are. Rolled up in an old sweatshirt, tucked in the back corner of my closet, and covered with shoes.

I need an excuse to head into town and this is it.

"I can go into town and grab some if you want?" I make a show of glancing at my watch. "It won't take me long and that way, the women will have the scent of lavender in their rooms when they arrive later today."

"That's an excellent idea." She squeezes my arm. "You're a good girl."

No, I'm not. I'm bad for deliberately deceiving my grandmother, and embarrassment scorches my cheeks.

"Be back soon," I say, injecting perkiness into my voice so she can't see that I'm a lying fraud.

She waves and resumes rummaging in the closet for more supplies, and I hightail it out of there. I'm consumed by the need to research genealogy sites and start of the process of hopefully finding extended family.

I know it's a long shot. Other members of Dad's family will need to have input their DNA into the database and ticked the boxes that they're willing to receive communication from matches. What are the odds?

But I have to try because understanding where my Dad came from might be the first step to helping him regain his memory and ultimately, control of his life. With the bonus of finding out more about Mom's family too.

An hour later, after stocking up on the candles, I'm at the library and scrolling through ancestry and family tree sites. Some are free, some aren't, but I can't input my credit card info because Gran scours the statements, so I choose a free service that promise the best results. I can't have the DNA kit sent to The Haven and risk Gran discovering what Dad and I are doing, so I put down Maisey's address. She won't mind and I'll remind her that discretion is paramount.

As I scour my entry in the database to ensure I've ticked all the right boxes, excitement skitters through me.

This is it.

The first step to discovering a family I never knew I wanted until the possibility was dangled in front of me. I'm hoping like hell it works out.

TWENTY-SIX

LEAH

THEN

A month after the twilight orchard party, Cora marries Harlan.

I should be happy but I'm not. Because I see the way Spencer still looks at her.

Yearning.

Hopeful.

Like he's not giving up.

That's okay, because I'm not a quitter either, and with Cora out of the picture technically, I have a real shot at happiness with Spencer.

Since our confrontation several weeks ago, the day that Cora dropped her marriage bombshell, our relationship has improved. I attempted to revert to being a light-hearted co-worker, he resumed his corny jokes and teasing. I try not to read too much into it, but I can't deny falling into our old pattern of laughter gives me hope.

Until today.

Cora may not be as clever as she thinks she is, because after the ceremony I see her in an intense exchange with Spencer.

And her hand drifts to her abdomen.

I stiffen and all the blood drains from my head to my toes. I sway and almost collapse onto the nearest chair.

She's pregnant.

And by the way Spencer's radiating fury, the baby could be his.

So that's why she married Harlan so quickly. She didn't want the paternity of the baby questioned and she didn't want to raise the baby with penniless Spencer, far from Arcania. For there's no doubt they would've been banished the moment her pregnancy became obvious.

Cora had married Harlan for money and security. I admire her putting her unborn child's needs first, but if that baby is Spencer's, I hate her too, because she's sentenced him to watching another man raise his child.

In that moment, the memory of losing my baby and the realization I'll never have another crash over me and I'm swamped by grief. My chest tightens and spots dance and coalesce before my eyes. I'm unable to rein in the tears, so I lurch to my feet and stagger into the orchard, blindly pushing branches aside.

I thought I'd dealt with my grief. I've made a new life for myself. I live with great girls. I'm working for the first time in my life and actually enjoying it. I'm independent and free of my parents. But maybe the thought of Cora having a baby when I never will has resurrected deeply suppressed sorrow.

"Leah? Are you okay?"

I should be happy Spencer saw my distress and had

come after me. But I'm truly blubbering now and as he envelops me into his arms and murmurs soothing words while stroking my hair, my desolation is complete.

He's comforting a friend, whereas I crave his touch for real. To be in his arms like this. For him to hold me and cherish me.

For him to look at me the way he looks at Cora.

That thought subdues my sobs, and I ease out of his arms. Sadly, he lets me go.

"What's going on—"

"Is Cora pregnant with your child?"

His jaw drops before it closes with an audible click. "What are you talking about?"

"That's why she married Harlan so quickly, because she's pregnant, and if it's yours, she wants to ensure there's no question of paternity."

His shoulders slump along with my hopes for us being anything more than friends, because if the baby is his, it will tie him to Cora for life. "I asked her. She denied it."

"You don't believe her."

It's a statement, not a question, and he shrugs.

"I have to."

Three words laced with longing and regret. And this time I want to comfort him. But he doesn't deserve it, not if he's still hung up on a woman who's not only lied to him, she's thrown anything they might've shared in his face.

"What are you going to do?"

He shrugs. "Keep working. Save as much as I can so I can get away from here."

"Good plan."

I want to tell him there's plenty of work in Edgewater Bay, ninety minutes from here. That it's a lovely town and I have a place he can stay if he needs it. But I'm not a masochist and my heart is already breaking. I'm better off biding my time and seeing if Spencer can get over her. Who knows, with time, we might have a chance?

It sounds pathetic even in my head but he's my first love. What else can I do?

"Leah, I want you to know I appreciate your friendship." He places a hand on my shoulder and squeezes, and my heart fractures a little more.

Friendship.

Yep, that's us. Buddies. Pals.

I'm an idiot.

But I say, "I'm here if you need me. Anytime."

When he embraces me I hold my breath, every cell in my body leaping to attention and straining toward him, wishing this hug means more.

It doesn't and all too soon he releases me, leaving me yearning more than ever.

TWENTY-SEVEN

RYLEE

NOW

I'm on a grocery run into town, my third this week, so I can pop into Maisey's to see if the DNA kit has arrived. Discreet as always, Maisey didn't seem surprised when I filled her in seven days ago: that I was researching my family in secret and to expect a parcel. I'm rapt to have re-established our friendship, and it's nice to have someone in my corner who's nonjudgmental.

Maisey's Marvels is empty as I step inside and the moment I see a smile on Maisey's face and a thumbs up, I know it's arrived.

"It's in the back," she says, flipping the 'closed' sign on the door.

"Great." I force a smile and swipe my sweaty palms down the side of my jeans, because now that the moment's arrived, trepidation makes me pause.

Do I really want to do this? Delve into a potential minefield?

"You don't have to proceed," she says, intuitive as ever, patting my arm. "I'm not going anywhere, so you can leave the parcel here and return any time you want."

Her understanding brings tears to my eyes and I blink them away. I've come this far. No point dithering now.

"I'm okay," I say, and with a nod, Maisey leads me into the back room where a small, nondescript brown paper box is sitting on a desk. I guess I'm not the only one who values discretion when it comes to tracing one's family tree and the DNA kit is packaged accordingly.

"I'll leave you to it," she says, with a smile. "Detox tea in ten minutes?"

"Perfect. Thanks."

I wait until she leaves the room before tearing off the wrapping and opening the plain white box. The instructions are simple and after swabbing the inside of my cheek and placing the plastic test-tube into a sealed bag I exhale the breath I'm unaware I'm holding. I double check I've done everything right and finally relax into the chair, just as Maisey comes bustling back into the room with a teapot and two porcelain cups on a tray.

"All good in here?"

"All good," I say. "You sure you don't mind mailing this for me?"

"Honey, the last thing you need is some busybody at the post office seeing the address on this envelope and you're the one sending it." She makes a blabbing motion with her hand. "You know how people in this town talk."

Actually, I don't. I've had limited contact with anybody other than Gran, Dad, Mel, Freda, their families, and The

Haven's guests, for years. But I can't risk gossip getting back to Gran about what I'm doing, so I'm playing it safe.

"Thanks, Maisey. I appreciate it."

"Not a problem." She pours tea into both cups and hands me one. "Did your gran tell you about Arcania?"

I shake my head. "She said she'd never worked at a wellness retreat."

A shrewd gleam lit Maisey's eyes. "Ah, but it wasn't a wellness retreat when she worked there, was it? It was an orchard."

"That's what I thought too. A lie by omission. But why lie at all?"

Maisey shrugs. "Who knows why people do half the things they do? Perhaps your grandmother is ashamed of working there for some reason and didn't want to admit the truth when you asked because it might invite other questions she doesn't want to answer."

"That makes sense."

But it doesn't make it any easier to accept. My grandmother is a staunch advocate for the truth. I've heard her tell The Haven's inhabitants many times that the truth will set them free.

So why is she lying to me, one of those closest to her?

"There's something else my friend told me about your grandmother and her obsession with Arcania."

Eager for whatever snippet I can learn, I ask, "What is it?"

"The main attraction of Arcania for Leah wasn't the mansion itself as much as a man."

Intrigued, I lean forward. "Do you have a name?"

Maisey shakes her head. "My friend couldn't remember, but she said Leah mooned around after him like a lovesick pup, and everyone knew it except the guy."

It's no biggie that Gran had a crush. It humanizes her in my eyes.

But why the secrecy?

Unless... "When you first told me about Arcania, you mentioned all the disappearances and deaths that occurred there. Was Gran's boyfriend one of those who vanished or died?"

"I don't know. But it might explain why she doesn't want to talk about it." Maisey grimaces. "Rehashing the past might be painful for her."

"Yeah..." I murmur, more determined than ever to see Arcania for myself and ferret out the hold it has over my grandmother, and why she's compelled to lie about it.

TWENTY-EIGHT

19 years later

LEAH

THEN

"Can I ask you something, Leah?"

Cora pours me a glass of lemonade. It's piquant and sweet, made with lemons from the orchards. Daphne has become a master in the kitchen over the years. Like Spencer and me, she's stayed way longer than any of us expected.

"Thanks." I accept the glass. "Sure, ask away."

"Why are you still here?"

The lemonade catches in my throat, and I cough to clear it. "Arcania is a great place to work," I say, my trite response not fooling her for a second.

"You've been here for nineteen years and by your clothes, you don't need to work."

Damn, I've been dressing down deliberately from the start, but Cora's too astute for her own good.

"It's the way you wear them, with an elegance that comes from being secure in your own skin," Cora says. "Harlan has that way about him. His parents had it too. Money breeds confidence." She gives a soft snort. "I'd like to think I have that too now."

Considering the Medville's died not long after I started working here nineteen years ago, making Harlan and Cora the master and mistress of Arcania, she's had a long time to get used to the wealth.

They're a strange couple and I can't fathom how obtuse Harlan is.

Can't he see what Cora and Spencer are doing?

As expected, my wishes for Spencer to quit pining for Cora and realize how good we can be together are futile. When Cora gave birth to a daughter, Ava, eighteen years ago, he was more smitten than Harlan. Sure, he did a good job of hiding it, but what Spencer didn't know was I watched him as obsessively as he watched Ava.

I wasn't sure whether to be appalled by his blind faith that Ava is his child despite Cora denying it or admiring that someone can have so much hope.

Then again, I've stuck around all these years because of hope, so which one of us is the bigger fool?

"You didn't answer my question, Leah."

Cora's subtle prompt wrenches me out of my reverie. "I'm not the only one who's worked here forever. What about Daphne and Spencer? You should be grateful for our loyalty."

My barb hits home, and she reddens. She knows I'm referring to Spencer, and we both know why he's stuck around all these years.

Cora and Spencer are lovers.

I see them sneaking glances occasionally when they think no-one is watching. But I'm always watching, and I can't believe their audacity.

If Harlan finds out, he'll kill them.

It won't be the first time he's committed murder.

Rumors were rife at the time his parents died, that he had a hand in the boat explosion that made him their sole heir, and there have been several disappearances since, employees that vanish without a trace. It's why I only work one day a week now. I may have reasons for maintaining a connection to Arcania, but I don't want to end up dead, and working on Harlan's day when he has meetings with suppliers in nearby large towns is no accident.

Personally, I think Spencer must have a death wish because if Harlan ever discovers he's sleeping with his wife, he'll be next to disappear.

Occasionally, when I'm lying in bed, listening to The Haven creak and groan around me in the middle of the night, my inherent loneliness clawing at me, I wonder if it would be better if Spencer wasn't around. But I'm not vindictive and there are easier ways not to pine for him; like quit working at Arcania.

Nobody would understand my rationale for working here for nineteen years, especially when I don't need to financially. Arcania is my escape from the everyday good-ness of my life, of helping countless homeless young people over the years; it's my guilty pleasure.

Seeing Spencer cast surreptitious glances at Cora once a week, hearing the workers' terrifying tales of their fellow employees disappearing, being immersed in the grandeur that is Arcania, makes me feel alive in a way that helping people at The Haven doesn't.

It's easy to be altruistic when you have money. But the feelings I harbor aren't always good and here at Arcania, being bad—even if it's only in my thoughts—makes me feel like I'm not so out of place.

Devious things happen here. People aren't what they seem.

I fit right in.

"I know why Spencer and Daphne have worked here so long, but you?" Cora's head tilts to one side as she studies me. "I can't figure you out."

"Maybe it's a habit?" I shrug, my offhandedness annoying her as her lips compress. "You're right. I have money, but I enjoy working part time. It keeps me from taking things for granted, you know?"

It's another barb because the day she married Harlan is the day Cora stopped working. She struts around on the pretext of managing the house and the employees, but everyone knows Daphne is the unofficial housekeeper of Arcania and Spencer manages the rest.

Either she chooses to ignore my petty jibe or she's tiring of my glib responses, because her expression softens as she tops up my lemonade. "I envy you."

I almost didn't hear her soft murmur and lean forward, my eyebrows shooting heavenward. "You envy me?"

She nods, gnawing on her bottom lip, wistful. "You're free."

Once again, her words are barely above a whisper, like she's fearful someone will overhear. We're not friends, never have been, but a small part of me feels sorry for her. The moment she married Harlan, she gave up any semblance of freedom. He's not a man to be crossed and as he's gotten older, his propensity to make my skin crawl has increased, which is why my work hours coincide with his absences.

"I know this isn't my place, but I assume you've stuck by Harlan all these years because of Ava?"

Cora's eyes widen, the truth reflected in their depths.

"But Ava's eighteen now. Surely the two of you can leave if you wanted to?"

She shudders, her face a mask of fear. "He'd find us..." she murmurs, shaking her head. "We shouldn't be discussing this."

I'm about to say more when I see Harlan striding toward us, his expression thunderous. He's returned early. He's flushed and his hands are clenched into fists at his sides. That's my cue to make myself scarce.

"Thanks for the lemonade. I'll be outside—"

"Cora, I need to speak with you. Now." Harlan's command is a bellow and Cora pales.

I almost ask if she wants me to stay, but we're not close and I don't want to get in the middle of an argument, not with Harlan's foul mood. I've stayed away from him after our earliest smarmy encounter many years ago, and I want to keep it that way.

When Harlan reaches us, he grabs Cora's arm and yanks her to her feet, not casting me a glance as he drags her toward the staircase. I scurry away, making a beeline for the corridor that leads to the kitchen and the back door. But Cora's cry of pain and "you're hurting me" makes my steps slow.

If rumors are correct, Harlan's disposed of many people over the years, including his parents.

Would he harm his wife?

I make a split-second decision. I duck into the small storage room in the foyer. It gives me an unimpeded view of the staircase, from top to bottom, so I see him drag her upstairs. When they reach the landing, he releases her, but he's towering over her, intimidating and terrifying. I can't hear everything that's being said, but when Harlan starts yelling, the words 'whore like her mother' drift down and I'm genuinely fearful for Cora.

As his shouting escalates and he hits her, I have to intervene. I open the door a tad wider, uncertain what to do, when I see them struggling, a second before Cora places both hands on Harlan's chest and shoves hard.

I swear she's smiling as he tumbles down the stairs to his death.

CHAPTER
TWENTY-NINE

RYLEE

NOW

I wish I could've paid to get the DNA test expedited. Patience isn't my virtue. But the site said it could take anywhere between eight to twelve weeks for results to show up, so I have no choice but to wait.

It's almost like Gran has a sixth sense when I'm up to something, because the day after I did the test at Maisey's and returned home with the candles, Gran gives me the monstrous task of remodeling the sunroom and back verandah with a view to adding more rooms to The Haven.

It takes up all my time—finding contractors, collecting quotes, choosing everything from floor tiles to faucets— and I barely have time to eat, let alone do anything else. While Gran makes the final decisions on everything, she's surprisingly generous with allowing me to do what I like with the renovations. She says it will look good on my résumé; if I ever get out of here to find a job, that is.

She's extra attentive toward Dad too, to the point of smothering. Ever since she learned he had that 'turn' one evening, she hovers over him. It validates our choice to keep Dad's returned memory a secret from her. She'd go nuts if she heard about that.

Following on from his memory of holding hands with a woman on a beach, he's had another memory resurface— holding a hammer and a tool belt—and like the first, it doesn't scare him. He feels comforted by it and I hope whatever else he remembers is as serene.

Dad knows I'm waiting for the DNA test results and any hits on the ancestry family tree site. He's more invested than me, considering what I find might have far-reaching consequences, particularly for him. If I discover any links to family, will it cause a chain reaction with his memories? Will he finally get answers to questions he may be too scared to ask?

Only one way to find out, and I'll do whatever it takes to protect him. I'm the one who's eager to learn more about our extended family and while he's supportive, he has a lot more to lose than I do: namely, the protective barrier his memories afford him.

I've been reading through Mom's letters and I'm up to my fourteenth birthday. The previous letters have been updates on her life, her job, and her love for me. I may resent her for staying away all these years, but I can't fault her dedication. In every letter she mentions our future and her hopes that we'll be reunited. I can't help but wish for the same.

The house is quiet, and the moonbeams dance across my bed as I curl up under a blanket on the floor and slide the next letter out of the envelope.

. . .

Dear Rylee,

I have a confession to make. I'm missing you so much that I got Freda to film some of your fourteenth birthday just so I can feel close to you.

You're so pretty, my darling. I loved the white sundress you wore for the celebration at The Haven. And you looked so happy (I'm sure you're a typical rebellious teen at times, but all I saw that day was joy.

You're special, my girl, and I hope you know that. It made my heart ache to see your father in the video too. He's still strikingly handsome. I know it's silly of me to wonder, but a small part of me hopes that one day we can all be reunited as a family. Freda tells me he's single and still a recluse, and while I wish him happiness, I'm also secretly glad. Not that I want him stuck in that house, but if he doesn't meet the love of his life, there's still hope for me.

Not that I've been single all these years. I've dated, and I've had one long-term relationship. George, a landscape gardener, was my boyfriend for fourteen months. But he wanted to have children and I can't. Not when I'm pining for you every single day. It would seem disloyal somehow to have more kids, like I've moved on.

Don't get me wrong, I'm not a martyr. But there isn't a day that goes by that I don't wonder what you're doing, how you're feeling, and wish that I was with you.

Freda says you're clever and I'm so proud. I wish you could attend high school rather than be homeschooled, but I know what your grandmother says goes. As for you working part-time, I hear that's off the table too. Freda says it's ironic, because even though Leah had money and didn't have to work when she first arrived in Edgewater Bay, she worked at an orchard about forty-five minutes away. She said Arcania was all Leah could talk about in those early days, and she worked there for almost twenty years before abruptly stopping, with no explanation. Typical Leah, mysterious and secretive. I really hope that once you turn eighteen, baby girl, you want to spread your wings and we can reconnect.

Anyway, please know I'm always thinking about you. I know you'll be tempted to ask Freda about me and maybe even ask her if we can get in contact, but I don't want her to get into trouble and if your grandmother finds out, she'll cut off Freda and then I'll have no updates on your life. Besides, all Freda has is a gmail address for me and I know you can't email from the home computer because she'll be monitoring. And Freda mentioned you aren't allowed to have a cell. Hopefully that changes when you're older and we can reconnect that way.

So we'll have to bide our time and I hope that one day we'll be reunited.

Love you,

Mom xx

I STARE at the letter in disbelief.

So Maisey was telling the truth about my grandmother's connection to Arcania.

And Gran was lying.

The next time I have a few free hours—which will be never if Gran has her way—I'm going to check out Arcania.

THIRTY

LEAH

THEN

Cora doesn't know I saw her kill Harlan and I keep it that way.

At the time I was equal parts horrified at her callousness and admiring of her bravado. And now, three weeks later, I know what they were arguing about.

Ava's pregnant.

She's quiet and subservient like her mother and has been all these years. Since childhood, she's drifted through Arcania, oblivious to those around her, her nose stuck in a book. Homeschooled and never allowed out, she's a prisoner in her own home. I've pitied her for years, but kept my distance because she's jittery and fearful of everyone.

Except Spencer.

They have an invisible bond that all but cements my suspicion they're biologically related. She's followed him around since toddlerhood and confided in him during her teens. The girl's intuitive, because she avoided Harlan whenever she could, and I don't blame her. We all sat through his funeral on the property. No surprise that Cora and Ava didn't shed a tear. Nobody did.

Since then, Ava and Spencer have been closer than ever. I still work Fridays and for the last few weeks I've seen them deep in conversation, Ava's hand unconsciously drifting to her belly, just like Cora's had at the same age. I don't know what Ava and Spencer are planning, but it's obvious Cora's not part of it.

"Hey Leah, do you have a minute?"

I dust off my hands—sorting potatoes means I won't get the dirt out from under my nails for a week—and smile at Sam, Ava's baby daddy if my suspicions are correct.

"Sure, Sam. What's up?"

He's hesitant and runs a hand through his mussed hair. I can see what Ava sees in him. He has an appealing surfer look—lean body, relaxed posture, easy smile, bright blue eyes, shoulder-skimming blond hair—and has a way of looking at you with intent focus.

"Why doesn't Spencer like me?"

We've chatted a few times before this. Sam's a nice young man, respectful and earnest, and not like the other workers who drift through here. He has plans for his life— picket fence, wife, kids, a mechanic business—and I admire his drive. I guess Ava does, too. Maybe that's what she sees in Sam, a way to escape Arcania?

But despite our occasional conversations, his question is from left field. I can't tell him the truth—that I'm guessing Spencer doesn't like him because he knocked up his daughter—so I settle for placating.

"Spencer has worked here a long time, and he's protective of Arcania and all those who live here."

Sam frowns. "Meaning?"

"He's close to Cora and Ava, and from what I've seen you like Ava?"

Understanding sparks his eyes and an endearing blush stains his cheeks. "Is it that obvious?"

I smile. "Young love often is."

His blush deepens. "I do love her. But it's complicated."

I wonder if he's talking about Ava's unnatural attachment to this place or the pregnancy. "Relationships often are."

"Her dad just died too, though from what she's told me, he was a mean SOB and she's not that cut up about it. But I want stability for her, for our uh..." Yeah, she's definitely pregnant, but he doesn't want to confide in me completely. "...relationship, so I want to stay here, build a future for us." He shakes his head. "But that Spencer dude seriously doesn't like me."

"Give him a chance," I say, but I agree. From what I've seen of their interactions, Spencer hates Sam. It's unnerving because Spencer is usually a gentle guy who's accepting of everyone. Which proves how protective he is of Ava and potentially sees Sam as a threat.

With Harlan out of the way, I presume Spencer sees him, Cora, and Ava becoming a happy family and if that's the case, he doesn't like Sam because he fears Ava will ultimately leave and take her baby—Spencer's grandchild—with her. Or perhaps it's the opposite, and with Sam wanting to stay, he'll tether Ava to Arcania and Spencer wants to help her escape?

"Thanks for the chat, Leah, but I have to get back to work."

"No problems."

But as Sam lopes away, I see one big problem: Spencer won't tolerate Sam standing in his way of the family he's always wanted.

RYLEE

NOW

The elaborate ruse I have to perpetuate in order to visit Arcania is ludicrous. Which other eighteen-year-olds have an overprotective grandparent like mine? I should be at college, drinking too much and staying up too late, not sneaking around like a fugitive.

I'm doing this for Dad, and ultimately, for me. I know that once I find Mom, I'll leave Edgewater Bay. But to do that, I need to know Dad will be okay and perhaps he can come too. Fear of the unknown—of his past—keeps him tethered to The Haven but if he recovers more memories and realizes they're not as terrifying as he thinks, I'm hoping it will give him the momentum he needs to break away.

Gran will freak out. And that's what's driving me to discover as much as I can about her past; because information is power. If I understand my grandmother better, I'll have a better chance of convincing her that my life is my own. Dad's too.

Depending financially on her is a problem and I want to find a part-time job ASAP. Not that she wouldn't give me money if I asked, but I need a safety net, something I can fall back on if needed. Besides, would she really give me money if it was for me to leave?

I arrive in Nag's Head just after eleven in the morning. Their annual Vegetable Growers Festival is in full swing, with rides for the kids, food stalls, and experts taking to the main stage to give lectures on everything from propagation to irrigation.

I'd played on Gran's plans to expand her vegetable garden at home by saying I was keen to help and wanted to learn as much as I can from the experts at the festival. Thankfully, she'd bought my excuse, giving me all day to visit Arcania, with Gran none the wiser.

I leave my car in Nag's Head—yeah, I'm being overly cautious in case Gran makes a surprise visit to the festival —and take the bus to Arcania, a fifty-minute trip. The bus stops about a mile away and I walk along the road, wrinkling my nose against the pungent mix of swamp and ocean brine.

I see the Arcania sign first, that vivid turquoise Viking compass against a white background. It's striking and I wonder what it would be like to check into a wellness retreat and digitally detox. Then again, considering I didn't have a cell until recently and don't spend a lot of time on the computer or watching TV, I'm pretty much doing the same thing at home.

As I walk up the driveway, I catch my first glimpse of Arcania. The mansion—with fifteen windows across two floors, whitewashed walls, and green trim—appears surprisingly unassuming. I'm not sure what I expected, but this place seems sedate for the rumors surrounding it. The photos online hadn't done it justice though because it gives off a stately aura not many homes do.

There's a boardwalk to my right, cutting through a swamp, and I suppress a shiver as I remember Maisey saying the owner's daughter had been taken by an alligator here. I steer clear.

There aren't any cars parked at the front, and there's no movement behind any of the windows. I expected to see a 'For Sale' sign from a realtor in the front too, but there's none. Then again, a place this size could be up for private sale only, so what's the point in advertising signage?

I follow a path around the mansion toward the back. There's an orchard on my left filled with apple trees and I wonder if that's where Gran worked, or did she work inside the main house? I still can't believe she worked here for almost two decades but denies it. Unless she knows something about all those disappearances and wanted to put the past behind her. Selective memory, like Dad. In which case, I can't blame her for that, but I thought we had the kind of relationship where she'd be truthful if I asked a question.

Instead, she's lied repeatedly, and I want to discover what it is about this place that's made Gran want to forget it.

The back garden is huge, a sprawling lawn with a gazebo on one side and a detached yoga studio on the other. The distant pounding of waves against sand is soothing and I can imagine city folk unwinding here, far from the manic pace of their hectic lives.

I glance at the mansion and from this angle, there's a definite eeriness and I rub my arms to ward off a smattering of goosebumps. It could just be my overactive imagination, but I feel I'm being watched, despite the abandoned vibe.

I'm not going to learn anything by wandering around, so I'll knock on the front door and see if anyone's here that I can subtly quiz.

However, as I wander back along the path toward the front of the mansion, I hear the slam of a car door and I pause at the corner of the house, in time to see my grandmother sitting on her car hood, arms wrapped around her middle, staring at Arcania like she's seen a ghost.

CHAPTER
THIRTY-TWO

LEAH

THEN

Ever since Harlan died, there's a pall hanging over Arcania. A darkness that makes goosebumps spring up at the oddest of times. It's strange, because I can live with the ghosts of witches past at The Haven, but the ominous fog seeping through every nook and cranny of Arcania is seriously freaking me out.

Oddly, it seems like only Spencer and I feel it. Cora is positively giddy since she shoved Harlan to his death. Well, not giddy exactly, but her demeanor is lighter than I've ever seen. She's lost the perpetual frown, and she smiles at everybody. Her euphoria at being a widow blinds her though.

She can't see how edgy Spencer and Ava are.

It makes me wonder if she knows about her daughter's pregnancy. Ava is Spencer's shadow these days; when she's not mooning over Sam, that is.

The two of them are cute together. I see them holding hands in the shade of the apple trees, their heads bent together as they whisper and smile, making secret plans. Maybe that's why Spencer's expression is thunderous more often than not, because he sees them too?

I try to ask him about it.

"Sam seems like a good kid."

Spencer grunts. "He should spend more time working and less time making eyes at Ava."

"They're young and in love. Don't you remember what that was like?"

I'm referring to the way he used to moon around after Cora and by the withering glare he shoots me, he knows it.

"Ava has her whole life ahead of her, a life that doesn't involve being trapped in this place." He scowls as he gestures to the mansion behind me. "She's been cooped up here long enough."

That's the moment I realize what Spencer and Ava's plotting could be about. Is he helping her get away from Arcania to have an abortion?

My stomach roils at the thought. If anyone knows what it's like to have parents interfere in a teen pregnancy, I do, and I'm still suffering the fallout nineteen years later. Because every time a kid walks through the doors of The Haven, I can't help but wish mine had lived.

The grief grips me sparingly these days, not like at the start when I clung to anything—including working here when I didn't need to—to distract. But it hurts just the same and I'm swamped by an unexpected surge of overprotectiveness toward Ava.

"Ava's eighteen and more than capable of choosing what she wants to do with her life," I say, my tone icy. "You should butt out."

Spencer gapes at me. "I know we've been friends a long time, Leah, but with all due respect, you know nothing about Ava's situation."

"I know enough. She's been locked away here like a princess in an ivory tower for her entire life. That's not normal. Trust me, I know..." I trail off, belatedly realizing I've said too much. Nobody at Arcania knows anything about my past, and I intend to keep it that way. Knowledge will invite questions I have no intention of answering.

"What does that mean?"

Of course he asks. Curiosity is written all over his face.

"Just that my parents were overprotective, and I ended up rebelling, which didn't end well. I don't want the same for Ava."

Mollified, he nods. "She's lucky to have people who care about her."

"She is. I only want what's best for her."

His expression softens, and he squeezes my arm. "You're one of the nicest people I know, Leah."

"And don't you forget it." I wink, and he chuckles as I walk away with a wave.

My chat with Spencer hasn't appeased me. He's up to something with Ava and I hope he's not convincing her to do something she doesn't want—like terminating her pregnancy—so I go in search of Ava. She won't appreciate me interfering, but if I can warn against making a mistake that might haunt her for the rest of her life, I'll do it.

I see her slipping out of one of the storage sheds, a huge grin on her face. A second later, Sam follows her, sporting the same smug grin. I'm happy for them and I hope their overt happiness means they're making plans for their future.

I wait until Sam disappears in the direction of the orchard before waylaying Ava.

"Can I chat with you for a minute?"

Ava's instantly on guard, her eyes narrowing slightly, but she nods. "Sure."

"I know this is none of my business, Ava, but I wanted to tell you if you're making plans for a future with Sam, I'm all for it." I glance around to make sure we're alone and can't be overheard. "I was in your position once, and I let me parents push me into making a decision I didn't want. Don't let that happen to you."

She gnaws on her bottom lip, as if she's torn between revealing the truth or saying nothing.

"Spencer is a good guy. I've known him since I started working here nineteen years ago, but if you have genuine feelings for Sam, he's your future and you should follow your heart."

It's the most I can say without revealing my teen pregnancy and the fallout, and that I know she's pregnant too and possibly being pressured by a father figure.

After an eternity, she smiles. "Thanks, Leah. I appreciate the advice."

"No worries. I'm here every Friday if you ever want to talk."

I know it's an offer she won't take me up on, but I feel like I've done my duty in warning her against whatever Spencer is trying to convince her to do.

With my shift over, I head home. The Haven is oddly quiet these days, with only one runaway staying, a seventeen-year-old boy who probably won't stay long. He keeps his duffel packed, like he'll bolt into the night. It's happened before, kids who only stay a few nights before moving on despite my reassurances they'll have a home here for as long as they need it.

I miss the days when The Haven was full. Mel and Freda were a great advertisement for the place and for several years every room in the house was occupied. But the girls have children of their own these days and while I love babysitting when they need me, seeing them with kids only reinforces I'll never have what they do.

Melancholic, I make an impulsive decision to take the boat out. A metal dinghy, really, that I rejuvenated after finding it in the shed years ago. When the house was packed with people, I'd take it out at dusk for respite. Now, I hope the wind in my hair and the gentle waves will quell my loneliness.

When I take the boat out, there's one place I go.

Arcania.

Not the mansion itself, but the coves that dot the shore-line further up the coast. The first time I'd done it, I liked seeing the mansion perched high on the cliffs. A house where I belonged, even if no-one within its walls knew the real me. That was about ten years ago, and I've been boating here ever since. Seeing Spencer diving from one of those coves that first time cemented my newfound love of the water.

I'd brought binoculars next time and while I don't always spot him in the cove, I've seen him enough times to anchor offshore and watch. Creepy and voyeuristic, maybe, but Spencer has always been my forbidden pleasure.

The briny tang of the ocean fills my nose as the motor-ized dinghy skims the water. I feel like I'm flying, all my worries blown away by the wind. As I near the familiar buoy, I cut the engine and drop anchor. The sun is hovering on the horizon, a fiery gold sphere, before it dips, and the muted mauve of dusk descends.

I pick up the binoculars and aim them at Spencer's Cove, as I call it. I twist the knobs to focus, and when the sandy shoreline comes into view, I wish I hadn't.

I see Spencer and Sam.

More precisely, I see Spencer trying to kill Sam.

CHAPTER
THIRTY-THREE

RYLEE

NOW

Gran doesn't stay long. She stares at the house for five minutes before getting back in her car and driving away. I'm relieved I didn't drive here, because how would I have explained my presence when she saw my car?

The look on Gran's face—anger, fear, regret—solidifies my suspicion that there's a lot she's not saying about her links to Arcania and I'm hoping to find someone here who can tell me more.

I barge up to the front door, lift the heavy brass knocker emblazoned with that weird compass emblem, and let it fall. Nobody answers and I do it again, disappointment making me slump. I'd assumed someone would be here, but what if the owners had put the place on the market and left?

It'll be hard for me to come up with another excuse to

return on the off chance someone will be here, and I hate that I've hit a dead end. For my grandmother to drive all this way to sit in front of a house for a few minutes...it's bizarre. Maisey said Gran had been obsessed with Arcania, and what I'd just seen proves it.

But why?

I'm about to trudge back up the driveway toward the main road when I hear whistling. It's loud and tuneless, and coming from the back of the house.

I follow the same path and spy an older man in his sixties in diving gear walking toward the mansion. He stops when he sees me and raises his free hand; the other is lugging tanks.

"Hey, what can I do for you?"

I smile and approach him. "Hi, I'm Rylee Smith. I'm interested in history and a friend of mine in Edgewater Bay told me about this place, so I thought I could check it out, if that's okay?"

He lowers his tanks to the ground. "We're not really open for visitors."

"I wouldn't take up much of your time, honest. Do you work here?"

He nods. "Worked here for over forty years." He thrusts out his hand. "Spencer Hadley."

His hand is icy as I shake it. "Pleased to meet you."

Very pleased, because if he's worked here that long, he'll know Gran.

"I hear this place is up for sale?"

His brow arches. "Why? You thinking of buying it?"

I chuckle at his snark, and he joins in. "Okay, Rylee Smith. Let me get changed and I'll answer whatever historical questions you have about Arcania."

"Thanks." My response is subdued, while inside I'm

doing a happy dance. What are the odds of running into someone who's worked here for so long and who would definitely know my grandmother?

"Wait out here, then I'll give you the grand tour."

Spencer's eyeing me like he doesn't quite believe my story and thinks I'll abscond with the silverware. Then again, I don't blame him for being mistrustful. If the rumors about this place are true, he's probably fielded visits from curious reporters wanting a scoop on the disappearances and deaths.

He takes a step toward the house, but he's staring at me in a way that's vaguely uncomfortable. "You look familiar. Have we met before?"

I shake my head. "This is my first time here and I don't get out much." I grimace. "Homeschooled."

"Strange," he mutters, still peering at me like he's trying to figure out a puzzle. "I guess being homeschooled fostered your love of history."

"Yeah," I say, relieved when he believes my lie and shrugs.

"I'll be back in a sec."

He lets himself into the house with an ornate brass key at odds with the modernity of the yoga studio and huge glass-walled dining room I can see. As a wellness retreat, this place is intriguing, a mix of old-world charm and contemporary.

The salty tang of the ocean tickles my nose as I wait for Spencer, who returns in record time. I feel he doesn't trust me.

"Right. Where do you want to start the grand tour?"

I feign nonchalance and gesture toward the trees to my right. "How about the orchard? My friend mentioned that's what this place was back in the day."

"That's right. Who's your friend?"

"Maisey Michaels. She has a shop in Edgewater Bay."

"Never heard of her." His eyes narrow slightly, appraising me. "What's her connection to Arcania?"

"I'm not sure. She just mentioned it when I told her I'd like to major in local history one day."

The lies are dripping off my tongue and I hope I'm not blushing.

He hesitates for a moment before giving a brief nod. "We had a lot of workers drift through here back then. She may have been one of them, though I'm pretty good with names and Maisey Michaels doesn't ring a bell."

He's given me the perfect opening to ask about other workers, particularly long-term ones like my gran. "Forty years is a long time to work for an employer. Anyone else who's worked here that long and lives locally that I can speak to?"

His jaw clenches, and he shakes his head. "Not that I know of."

I want to ask if he knew Leah Smith, but if Gran's hiding her links to this place, there could be a reason and I don't want to tip him off. Who knows, things may have ended badly for my grandmother here, or worse, and I need to be subtle in my quest for information.

"Can I see the orchards please?"

He nods and leads me through row upon row of fruit trees in good upkeep. "Arcania was the biggest orchard in North Carolina in its day. We supplied fruit and vegetables far and wide. But when Harlan Medville passed away, his wife Cora transformed the place into a wellness retreat."

"The orchard appears well maintained."

"We had a gardening crew come through recently, before the place was handed over the realtor." He gestures at the mansion, whose rooftop is barely visible through the trees. "Though there's a lot to be packed away in the house. It's a massive job."

He pauses. "You wouldn't be interested in some part-time work, would you? We're desperate for help, and what could be more intriguing to a history hound like yourself than foraging around the old mansion?"

Gleeful, I'm about to respond when he holds up his hand. "Not that I'm encouraging you to be nosy, but Arcania is fascinating and the faster the place is tidied up the quicker it sells and I can join my granddaughter in Manhattan."

Gran will have a fit if she hears I'm working part time here, but what better way to get her to admit the truth?

"Actually, I am looking for work and I'd love to help get Arcania shipshape."

"Great." His smile takes years off his weatherworn face. "Lucy, the new owner, will want to interview you, but I'm sure it's a formality. Can you come back tomorrow evening at six?"

"I'll be here. Thanks."

"Don't thank me yet. You'll need to flex some serious muscle to get the inside of the mansion packed away."

"Can I see it now?"

The oddest expression flickers across his face, reluctance tinged with suspicion, as if he's still not buying my eagerness. He glances at his watch and shakes his head. "I'm expecting a call from my granddaughter's lawyer. Can we finish the tour tomorrow when you come for the interview?"

"Sure," I say, but as we make our way out of the orchard and Spencer bids me farewell before rushing into the house,

I have the strangest feeling he can't get rid of me fast enough.

THIRTY-FOUR

LEAH

THEN

I break every speed limit on the road to return to Arcania.

Thankfully, I'm not pulled over by the police and I make it to the mansion in eighty minutes, a record. I've never returned to work after a shift, but tonight warrants it.

I need to confront Spencer.

I pull into the driveway at Arcania in a spray of gravel and I've barely killed the engine before I'm running for the orchard. Tonight is the usual Friday night employee party in the orchard, and that's where everyone will be. Even Cora pops in since Harlan died and a small part of me admires her for trying to bond with her workers in a way her arrogant husband never had.

As I round the back corner of the house, I almost run into the man I'm looking for.

"Whoa." Spencer's hands shoot out and grip my arms to steady me. "What are you doing back here?"

"I need to talk to you."

His eyebrows shoot up as his gaze drifts over me. I know I must look a fright, with my windblown hair from being out on the water and my eyes wide with shock. I've never been any good at hiding my emotions.

"Want to come inside?"

I shake my head. The last thing I want is to be alone with this man. The man I've secretly loved for almost two decades. The man I thought was caring and gentle.

The man who's a killer.

But I can't alert him I know what he's done, not yet, so I say, "I'm really thirsty. If the punch isn't spiked tonight, I'd love some."

He doffs an imaginary cap and smiles. "Coming right up."

I marvel at his ability to behave completely normally after what I witnessed and the enormity of what he's done hits me. I've been running on adrenalin since I boated back to The Haven, got in my car, and sped straight here, and now it's wearing off I start to tremble. My knees wobble and I sink onto the nearest step, spots dancing before my eyes. Unsteady, I cup my hands over my mouth and take deep breaths, grateful when the wooziness eases.

The last thing I need is to pass out around a maniac.

"Hey, are you okay?" Spencer sits beside me on the step and hands me a cup of punch. "You don't look so good."

"What every woman wants to hear."

I'm annoyed at myself for trading our usual banter at a time like this. Then again, it's better if he thinks everything is normal between us, so I can blindside him with the truth and gauge his reaction.

Not that I'm going to accuse him to his face. I'm not that stupid. But I want to give him a chance to explain, to tell the truth. If he doesn't, I know what I must do.

Walk away from Spencer and Arcania without looking back.

If he doesn't trust me enough after all these years, I'll know he's not the man I thought he was and I don't want to become his next victim.

Confronting a potential madman isn't on my agenda.

"I'm worried about you, Leah." He reaches out and smooths a strand of hair off my forehead before tucking it behind my ear, and I sigh.

How can this man be a monster?

I drink to ease the tightness in my throat. Coming back here was foolish. I feel too much for Spencer to believe he's capable of hurting anybody.

"What's going on?" Spencer folds his arms and rests them on his knees. It draws my attention to his hands— long fingers, broad palms, light dusting of hair on his knuckles—and I can't believe he used them to submerge Sam in the ocean.

Sam, who can't swim.

I remember the day Sam told me. A bunch of workers had been badgering him to join them for a swim on a day off and he'd balked. I'd teased him about looking like a surfer but not wanting to go near the water, and he'd told me he was petrified of being out of his depth. I'd felt bad at the time, because I've never been a big fan of the ocean either and we'd laughed about it when I said his secret was safe with me.

Not so secret, considering Spencer must've found out about it and used it to get rid of Sam.

"I chatted to Ava earlier today."

He immediately stiffens. "What about?"

"Her plans."

His eyes narrow. "I thought we've already discussed this, and it's got nothing to do with you."

"I care. Nothing wrong with that." I pause, observing him carefully. "What will you do if she moves in with Sam?"

He's good, I'll give him that much. He's expressionless, but I glimpse a flicker of fear in his eyes and the slightest clenching of his fingers where they rest on his knees.

"Sam is irrelevant to Ava's plans," he says, his voice barely above a growl. "He wants to stay here, so he'll only hold her back if she wants to leave."

That's the moment I know why he killed Sam.

Spencer wants Ava to escape, and Sam would tether her here.

"You want her to leave," I say, eyeballing him. "That's what you've wanted all along."

He nods and looks away, unable to hold my gaze. "She can't stay here." Goosebumps pepper my skin when he adds, "It's not safe."

"Is Sam around?"

He must hear something in my voice, a hint of accusation, and his gaze flies to mine. "No. I had a talk to him earlier, and he's gone."

"He left?"

Spencer hesitates for a second before nodding. "He's not coming back."

"But he loves Ava. Why would he leave?"

"Because I made him see sense." Spencer leaps to his feet. "Why are you obsessed with this? Ava and Sam's relationship has nothing to do with you."

"So you've said." I stand, grateful my legs are stronger now. "We've been friends a long time, Spencer, and I care about you." I lay a hand on his arm. "Is there anything you want to tell me?"

This is it, the moment he'll prove how much he trusts me by confiding in me.

I'll reassure him his secret is safe with me and he'll realize just how important I am in his life. Who knows, it may be a turning point for us and he'll see me in a new light, as a woman who loves him so much she'll do anything to keep his secret.

There's a glimmer of suspicion in his eyes as he scans my face. "Like what?"

Two words that drive a stake through my heart.

Spencer's not going to confide in me.

He doesn't have feelings for me.

He doesn't feel anything, considering what he's done to Sam.

I have two options.

Report him to the police or walk away from him once and for all.

I can't stand to be near him, not after what he's done, and my skin prickles like a million ants are marching all over me. Nausea swamps me and I blink rapidly to stave off the sting of tears.

I've wasted nineteen years of my life on this man, hoping he'll finally *see* me. So having him fling the opportunity for us to bond forever in my face is the wake-up call I need.

Telling the police what I saw will result in a he said/she said scenario that will have no outcome if they can't find Sam's body. Even then, what does it prove?

Worse, reporting Spencer to the police may label me as crazy.

How will I explain that I happened to be watching the

shoreline near Arcania through binoculars at the same time Spencer drowned Sam?

That I left my workplace and boated back at the end of my shift?

That I'm wealthy yet continue to work on a Friday when I don't need to, at a place I've stuck around for nineteen years?

It sounds insane and who will the police believe, a respected employee who Cora will vouch for, or a woman who's so obsessed with Arcania she spies on it in her downtime?

"Leah?"

Spencer touches my arm, and I jump and take a step back.

"You're not acting like yourself." He points to the mansion behind me. "I think you should stay here tonight."

A hysterical laugh bursts from me, and I take another step back. "No thanks. I'm going home."

My irrational behavior doesn't impress him and his lips thin in disapproval. "Are you sure that's wise?"

Wiser than staying here and being murdered in my sleep.

Not that Spencer has any reason to harm me. Unless my less than subtle probing has alerted him to the fact I know what he's done and he'll do whatever it takes to shut me up too.

"Goodbye, Spencer."

I fight the urge to go to him, to hug him, to blurt how much he's meant to me for all these years. This man has been my world, even if he doesn't know it.

But he's not the man I thought he was, and I can't stand to be near him for a moment longer.

"Leah, stay—"

"Goodbye."

I'm relieved when he lets me walk away and when I reach my car and glance over my shoulder for a final glimpse of the man I love but should hate, I see him staring after me in a way that has me wanting to break into a run.

THIRTY-FIVE

RYLEE

NOW

B y the time I catch the bus back to Nag's Head to pick up my car, I'm famished, so I enter the first cafe I see to order a quick snack.

The Outlier is bright and cheerful—bleached walls covered in splashes of modern art, navy trimmed windows, red cushions on the white iron seats, buoys in every corner —with a distinct nautical theme. The aroma of sizzling bacon wars with roasted coffee beans, and I salivate.

I wait until the woman in front of me orders a freshly squeezed carrot and apple juice and moves aside before stepping up to the counter. The guy taking the orders is about my age, with a scruffy man-bun perched at a jaunty angle on top of his head, dark stubble, and a dimple when he smiles at me. Cute.

"What can I get you?"

"A BLT and a banana smoothie to go, please."

"Coming right up." He winks as I hand over my money. "You new to town or passing through?"

"Passing through. I heard that old gothic mansion Arcania was on the market and I'm a history buff, so wanted to check it out."

"Cool," he says, but he's already looking at the customer behind me, so I step aside to wait for my order.

"Excuse me." The woman who'd been in front of me in the queue taps my shoulder and I turn to see her eyeing me with curiosity. "I wasn't eavesdropping, but I heard you say you visited Arcania?"

Wary, I nod. "That's right."

"I worked there until recently." She holds out her hand. "Moon. I'm a yoga instructor."

"Rylee. Nice to meet you." I shake her hand, unable to believe my luck. Here's someone else I can grill for information. "How long did you work there?"

"A few years." She strikes a namaste pose. "Lucky for me, people who attend a wellness retreat are more than willing to try yoga." She smiles and I swear serenity radiates off her. "Besides, without access to screens, bored folks will try anything once."

I chuckle and she joins in.

"So you're interested in the history of Arcania, huh?"

I nod. "Yeah, local history is my passion. I'm intrigued by it."

"Well, Arcania's got that in spades." Her smile fades. "It's sad what happened to Cora though, and now her granddaughter is selling the place."

"My condolences. Did you know her well?"

Moon shrugs. "She was a good boss. Aloof, though. Kept to herself. Didn't have any friends, apart from Spencer."

"I met him."

She smiles. "He's a good guy. Can't do a downward dog pose to save his life, though."

We laugh again and I'm relieved she's vouched for Spencer. I hate to admit it, but my sheltered upbringing means I'm not the best judge of character. I resent Gran for that. Her overprotectiveness means I'm gullible, so I'm always wary of others. Apart from Maisey, who helped me through those tough mid-teen years, I don't have any friends.

Sure, Mel and Freda are a constant in my life, but they're Gran's friends. Thinking about Freda reminds me I need to see her. She can tell me more about Mom. I'm annoyed she's never reached out to me, to let me know about the letters and the regular contact with my mother, but I understand. Mom would've made her swear not to push me, to let me make my own decisions regarding reestablishing a relationship with her, and I should respect her for that.

"What's the new owner like?"

A tiny frown appears between Moon's perfectly plucked brows. "I only met her once, when she informed me she was selling Arcania. She seems nice enough."

Moon's not telling me everything. She's fidgeting with the label on her prepackaged oatmeal bar, and she's glancing over my shoulder as if she can't wait to grab her order and go.

To prompt her to divulge more, I say, "I'm having an interview with her tomorrow."

Moon's eyebrows arch. "An interview? But the place is closed."

"Spencer said they need help with packing up the inside of the mansion."

Moon hesitates, before nodding. "I guess that makes sense."

"A carrot and apple juice to go," bellows the guy behind the counter, and Moon says to me, "That's my order."

I step aside so she can grab her takeout cup, wishing I'd had more time to interrogate about Arcania.

She sips at her drink and raises it in my direction. "Nice to meet you, Rylee."

"You too," I say, with a smile.

Her hand is on the doorknob when she pauses. "Just be careful at Arcania, okay? Weird stuff happens there sometimes. People disappear."

There's genuine fear in her eyes as she hurries out the door, leaving me with residual goosebumps.

THIRTY-SIX

LEAH

THEN

After I turn my back on Spencer and Arcania for good, I find my son.

It's one of those paradoxes. Your heart breaks in a bad way, only to shatter in a good way.

Never in my wildest dreams did I think this would happen. A small part of me has wished that one of the kids who walk through the front door of The Haven in search of sanctuary would be like the child I'll never have, but it's been nineteen years since my parents forced me into giving birth to a baby that died—inadvertently rendering me infertile—and that's a long time to hold on to hope.

He's sitting in the living room at The Haven, bewilderment in his blue eyes, like he's unsure how he got here. I know the moment I see him he's the one, the kid to take the place of the one I'll never have. His eyes have the same haunted look as mine. He needs me. And maybe I need him too.

"Here's your coffee." I hand him a mug and he smiles his thanks. He takes it like me: no cream, no sugar. "Are you sure I can't fix you something to eat?"

"I'm good, thanks."

He takes a sip, then gulps the hot coffee. I want to warn him to take it easy or he'll scald his mouth, but it's not my place to tell him what to do. Those that stay here need to feel safe, not bossed around.

He has no bag, but that's okay. I learned long ago to keep a fully stocked wardrobe with various sizes for those that turn up here seeking refuge. I'm known in town for it, and while I buy new underwear and clothing most of the time, the second hand shop in Edgewater Bay always keeps their good stuff for me too.

He drains the coffee mug and stares into the bottom like he's trying to do a psychic reading on the dregs. His brow is still creased in bewilderment and his eyes have an oddly glazed quality.

"What's your name?"

He blinks several times, before murmuring, "I don't know."

That's strange. I've had a few drop-ins over the years who profess amnesia, only to find they're wary of me and would prefer not to share any details of their lives, but even those tell me their name.

My heart aches as he glances around the room, his perturbation increasing. Whatever's happened to this kid, he's been through a lot. He's late teens, early twenties at the most, and while I'm not exactly ancient at thirty-seven, I feel old most days. Watching kids like Mel and Freda grow up and have children of their own leaves me lamenting what I lost the day I gave birth to a dead baby who would've been whisked away for adoption regardless, and wishing things could be different.

"I can't remember anything." He presses his fingertips to his temples. "I don't know how I got here."

His foot taps against the floorboards and he's visibly nervous as his gaze darts around, seeking an escape. I don't think he's faking the amnesia, unlike the others, and I'm not sure how to handle him.

"Would you like me to take you to a doctor?"

The foot tapping increases until he eventually nods. "Yeah. I don't like feeling this way. Like I'm...untethered."

"Okay, I'll drive you." I stand and pick up my keys from the sideboard. "Do you know where you are?"

He shakes his head and stands too. After an eternity, he whispers, "I don't know anything..."

The tears in his eyes make me want to hug him tight, but he's jittery enough without having a stranger embrace him.

I call ahead and book an appointment with the doctor, and that seems to pacify the kid a little. Though he doesn't speak for the entire trip into Edgewater Bay and I don't ask him any more questions. I'd be agitated too if I couldn't remember a thing.

When we arrive at the medical center and I switch off the engine, I turn to him. "When I made the appointment, I had to give them a name, so I said John Smith." I press a hand to my chest. "My surname is Smith." I don't add that I used John in reference to John Doe. "I hope that's okay?"

He shrugs. "It's as good a name as any."

He's pretending to be strong, but I see a vein pulsing near his temple and his fingers are drumming against his thigh.

"It'll be okay," I say softly, reaching out to touch his shoulder. He doesn't flinch, thankfully, but he opens the car door and gets out.

After a ridiculously long wait to see the doctor and a thirty-minute examination which I'm not privy to, John rejoins me in the waiting room.

"The doctor wants to see you," he says.

"Is that okay with you?"

"Yeah, it's fine." He slumps into a chair like the entire process has exhausted him. "I'll wait here."

Doctor Sengham has been practicing medicine for thirty-eight years and while his bedside manner is brusque, he's thorough and practical, qualities I admire in a doc.

He beckons me into his office and gestures to a seat. "This won't take long, Leah, but I thought it best we speak in private."

I sit. "I know you can't give me details about John, but what are we dealing with?"

"That's what I wanted to talk to you about." He sits behind his desk and crosses his arms. "You've been an amazing asset to this town, Leah, taking in those less fortunate and giving them a good life, but John's case is complex, and you might be taking on too much with him."

I bite back my first response, 'that's for me to decide', and ask, "Why do you say that?"

"I think John is suffering from dissociative amnesia." He steeples his fingers and rests his elbows on his desk. "It's a result of a traumatic event, causing the person to block out memories and personal information. It's not the same as simple amnesia, which involves a loss of information from memory, because with dissociative amnesia the memories still exist but are deeply buried in the person's mind but can't be recalled."

Sadness fills me. What has John gone through to make him deliberately forget everything?

"Will he ever remember who he is and what happened to him?"

Dr. Sengham shrugs. "Memories can resurface on their own, or might be triggered by something in the person's surroundings. But some experts think buried memories might not be true and warn against trying to help a patient recover false traumatic memories."

The doc is right. This sounds like a lot to handle. But John needs me.

I know it's crazy to think we have some kind of bond, but I felt it the moment he entered The Haven.

John is the child I never had and never will.

Not that I'll ever tell anyone what I'm thinking, manufacturing a connection to a young man in the hope he'll become a surrogate son. It sounds nuts even in my thoughts. But I've helped so many people over the years. What's one more?

John's different and deep down, I know it. I've never taken this much of a personal interest in one of my strays before and I need to tread carefully, especially after what the doc said about him recovering traumatic memories.

Who knows what that might mean for all of us?

THIRTY-SEVEN

RYLEE

NOW

I swear I have a newly awakened guardian angel because I don't have to come up with another excuse where I'm going this afternoon because Mel calls Gran, desperate for a babysitter and she won't be back until late.

It gives me plenty of time to get to Arcania for my interview with Lucy at six. I drive this time, safe in the knowledge Gran won't be making any weird pit stops to stare at the mansion again.

She'd been in bed by the time I got home from Nag's Head last night, citing a migraine. Gran never gets headaches, let alone migraines, and it makes me even more curious. Was her visit to Arcania so traumatic she needed time to recover afterward?

It looks like my dad isn't the only one with painful

memories he's trying to suppress. The big difference is Dad can't remember; Gran doesn't want to.

It makes me more determined to work at Arcania. What better way to discover Gran's secrets than being in the place she's lying about?

Besides, I need something to keep my mind occupied while I wait for those damn DNA results. I'm popping into town tomorrow to check the ancestry website in the library, but I know it's too soon. I'm also dropping in on Freda to discuss Mom.

I know I could devour the rest of her letters and get to the last one where I'm hoping she's left her contact information, but rationing the letters is something I have to do. Reading snippets of her life over the years, getting a feel for who she is as a person, means I'll be ready when the time comes to meet face to face.

That day can't come quick enough.

I wish I could chat to Dad about all this, but I'm worried. If he's recovering his memory, the last thing he needs is for me to dump my problems on him. Though I know he'd want to hear what I'm going through, a small part of me is scared he'll articulate what I'm thinking: that I'm vacillating, wanting to find my mother, wanting to leave The Haven and spread my wings, wanting to know more about our extended family, wanting to discover Gran's secrets.

It sounds crazy just thinking about it, but I want to do this my way.

Dusk descends as I park outside Arcania. Mauve streaks a sky deepening to navy and casts shadows over the mansion. Pretty but eerie, at odds with my visit yesterday when I didn't feel this sense of...foreboding.

Thinking about Gran and her connection to this place must've put fanciful ideas into my head, and I shake out my arms and legs as I get out of the car and close the door. Living at The Haven means I have a healthy respect for otherworldly stuff, considering the occasional banging door, creaking floorboard, and icy presence I've encountered over the years. So it stands to reason a house that has stood here for centuries may have more than its fair share of ghosts.

I don't believe in curses but the tragedies that dog the owners here make me wonder if that's the main reason Lucy is selling Arcania. If I were her, I wouldn't want to tempt fate.

I've worn black pants, ankle boots, and a silky white shirt for the interview. Simple yet professional. Gran isn't a big fan of makeup, but she said little when Dad ordered me a massive lipstick/eyeshadow/blush kit online for my eighteenth birthday. Nor did she chastise me too much when she saw me watching makeup tutorials online, other than to say I'm pretty enough without all that gunk on my face.

I sometimes think Gran belongs in another century, but I love her, so I tolerate her idiosyncrasies. She's compassionate and understanding of those that have come through The Haven's doors over the years, yet she holds Dad and me to a different standard. In my father's case, he's toed the line because he's terrified of what he may find if he re-enters the big, bad, world. But for me, Gran's over-protectiveness is increasingly constricting and that's what nailing this job interview is about.

I want to work.

I want my own money.

I want a life away from The Haven.

Gran won't like it, but if I land this job, it's a fait accompli. Besides, Dad will be on my side. I think that's what the makeup gift had been about, the first step in giving me permission to be a grownup.

I raise the brass knocker on the door and let it fall. I don't have to wait long. Spencer opens the door, a welcoming smile on his face.

"Nice to see you again, Rylee." He glances at his watch. "Right on time."

"My grandmother is big on punctuality, so she's drilled it into me."

I'm tempted to ask if he knows Gran, but it's too much too soon. Time enough for questions when I'm working here and get to know him better.

"Wise woman." He gestures me in. "Lucy's waiting for you in the office."

I struggle not to gape as I enter Arcania's foyer. Polished parquet floors shimmer from the light cast by brass sconces on the walls, blood-red chaises are well spaced, velvet drapes in the deepest purple cover the windows, and a massive black wrought iron staircase bisects the foyer. It's gothic to the extreme and at odds with the modernity of the yoga studio and huge dining room I glimpsed out the back on my first visit yesterday.

"The previous owners tried to preserve the history of the mansion here in the foyer, but most of the place is renovated." Spencer's pride is audible. "It's impressive, huh?"

"Sure is." I've always loved the old-world vibe of The Haven, but Arcania trumps it.

He knocks on a door in a corner of the foyer and when it opens, a young woman in her mid-twenties smiles at us. She's wearing a similar outfit to me, but her blouse is green.

"You must be Rylee?" She holds out her hand and I shake it. "I'm Lucy Phillips, the new owner of Arcania. Please come in."

"Good luck," Spencer murmurs, before fading into the background as Lucy closes the door.

Driving here, I hadn't been nervous at all, mainly because Spencer assured me yesterday this interview was merely a formality. Then why wish me luck?

"Take a seat," Lucy says, indicating a caramel suede sofa in front of a fireplace, where she sits.

She must sense my surprise at the informality, because she laughs. "I don't feel comfortable sitting behind my grandmother's desk, so let's have our chat over here."

"I'm sorry for your loss," I say, as I sit on the sofa, with a cushion space between us.

"Thanks. I didn't know her well and was surprised to inherit Arcania."

"So that's why you're selling it?"

She nods, her expression shuttered. "I have no real connection to the place and my home is in Manhattan. You're local?"

"I live in Edgewater Bay, about ninety minutes from here."

Her eyebrow arches. "That's a long way to drive for a part-time job. Why do you want to work here?"

"I'm not sure if Spencer told you, but I'm a history buff, and Arcania fascinates me. I was snooping around yesterday, and when Spencer discovered my interest, he offered me the job. If you approve, that is."

She studies me, but rather than feeling uncomfortable, I'm oddly at ease. "You know the work will be boring, right? Packing up this office and the other rooms."

"That's fine. My grandmother runs a halfway house for the homeless, so I'm used to cleaning, tidying, that kind of thing, over the years."

"Your grandmother must be special to do that."

"She is." I almost blurt, 'she used to work here too', but Lucy won't know her. Spencer is the person I have to interrogate once we build a rapport. "When do you need me to start?"

"Movers are coming in a few days to take away some of the furniture and put it into storage, so it opens up the place and gives the illusion of space for prospective buyers, so perhaps you can start next week?"

"Sounds good."

She stands, ending the interview, which was the formality Spencer said it would be. It makes me wonder why I had to meet Lucy at all. "If you have any questions don't hesitate to ask Spencer. He's practically an institution around here."

I smile. "Thanks. He mentioned he's worked here for forty years. He must be sad to leave."

The oddest expression crosses her face: fear. It almost matches what I'd seen on Gran's face when I'd unwittingly caught her staring at the mansion yesterday.

What is it about Arcania that has a strange hold over people?

"I think Spencer's looking forward to a new start, too."

I pick up on the 'too', meaning Lucy's planning a new life also. Interesting.

"Will I see you next week?"

She shakes her head. "I'll be back in New York, but you never know. I might pop down if we get a buyer."

"Good luck. I hope it sells quickly."

"Me too."

We shake hands again and I get the weirdest feeling, like we've met before. Great, now this place is giving me the spooks, too.

Spencer's in the foyer when Lucy opens her office door

and I give him a thumbs up sign. He smiles and approaches. "Congrats on getting the job, Rylee. When do you start?"

"Next week," Lucy and I say in unison, and we laugh.

"See you then," I say, and after we bid farewell and I walk to my car, my back prickles with the feeling I'm being watched. But when I glance over my shoulder, the front door is closed and the windows are shrouded in darkness.

THIRTY-EIGHT

LEAH

THEN

"John's a great guy," Freda says, as we sit on the back porch of The Haven watching him weed the garden. "Though it's sad he can't remember anything."

"Yeah, it's been a month, and nothing." I shake my head. "Considering what the doc said, that he's probably blocked out a traumatic event, maybe it's a good thing?"

Freda shudders. "I'd hate to forget my life."

"That's because you married your hunky fisherman, have two amazing kids, and love what you do."

Freda glances at me, gratitude in her eyes. "And I have all that because of you. Letting me stay at The Haven for years, funding my part-time hospitality course, buying the food truck for me..." She places her hand over mine. "You're incredible, you know that, right?"

Emotion swells in my chest, making breathing difficult, and I gulp half my iced tea. "I only funded that truck because you make the best fish and chips this side of the Atlantic and how else would I get my fix once you moved out?"

Freda squeezes my hand and releases it. "I think you're amazing and I know everyone who you've welcomed into The Haven over the years feels the same way."

"It's too big for one person," I say, uncomfortable with her praise. "Besides, the ghosts need other occupants to hassle besides me."

Freda's eyes widen slightly. "So the weird stuff still happens?"

"A few slamming doors and creaky floors don't scare me."

I've seen worse. Much worse.

It's been four weeks since I walked away from Spencer, and Arcania, for good. I emailed Cora my resignation and she'd called twice. I didn't answer. Considering what she did to Harlan, those two deserve each other. Two murdering peas in a pod.

Not that it's been easy. I still think about Spencer, wondering what he's doing, if he's guilt ridden at all. But he's not my problem anymore, even if he haunts my dreams most nights.

Besides, I've got more important things to worry about. John is an incredible kid—I peg his age around late teens, early twenties—and I've spent a lot of time researching amnesia. I'm no expert, but I wonder if recovering his memories will be good for him considering why he blocked them out in the first place.

I've tried some gentle probing techniques I read about online to see if he remembers anything. It only resulted in John becoming agitated so I backed off. He'll recall what he needs to in time. Until then, we both need to be patient.

"Speaking of scary stuff, did you hear about that girl being taken by an alligator up the coast?" Freda's nose crinkles. "Nothing left of her but a finger."

"Gruesome."

Freda shoots me a concerned glance. "I wasn't sure I should say anything, considering it happened where you used to work."

Fear makes my hand shake as I place the glass I'm holding on the table. "Arcania?"

Freda nods. "Yeah, it happened in the swamp there."

I'd hated that swamp and avoided it, never understanding some of the employees fascination with it. They'd found it intriguing, how the mansion was bracketed by a swamp at the front and side, with the ocean at its back. But there was something malevolent about it, like it oozed a dark presence. Fanciful? Maybe, but it gave me the creeps.

Freda tut-tuts. "I feel sorry for the owner, considering she lost her husband then her daughter not that long after."

The iced tea I've consumed rises in my gullet and I swallow it down with effort as realization hits. "Ava Medville is the girl who was taken?"

"Yeah." Freda pats my arm. "That's why I popped in, because I thought if you hadn't read the news online yet it's better you hear it from me."

"Thanks for being so considerate," I say, struggling to hide how badly I'm reeling from this news.

Ava's dead.

Sweet, unassuming, naive, Ava.

I can't believe it.

Arcania is tainted by death. All the disappearances. The deaths. Harlan's parents. Harlan. Sam. And now Ava.

There's one common dominator.

Spencer.

But I refuse to believe the man I loved for two decades is a serial killer.

Besides, he wouldn't hurt Ava. He adored her. Hell, he killed Sam to help her escape Arcania. And how would he have done it, waited until an alligator happened to come along then shove her in the swamp?

No, I'm jumping to conclusions. And I've never been gladder to have turned my back on that awful place.

"Are you okay?" Freda tops up my iced tea and hands me the glass. "Here, drink this. You look like you need it."

"Thanks." I down the tea in several gulps. It does little to sooth the burning in my throat.

John glances toward us at that moment, his eyes crinkling in the corners as he smiles and removes his gardening gloves, and the tightness in my chest eases.

I need to forget Arcania and its inhabitants and focus on the here and now.

John needs me and I'm better off helping him regain his memories and getting on with his life than worrying about the ghosts of my recent past.

THIRTY-NINE

RYLEE

NOW

I haven't broken the news about my job to Dad or Gran yet, because I need to head into town to check the ancestry website and see Freda, and I know that won't happen once my grandmother learns I'll be working at Arcania.

She barely spoke two words to Dad and me over breakfast when she's usually garrulous, and I'd caught her staring out the back window a few times, lost in thought. One of our current occupants needed to see a social worker and Gran had taken them to Nag's Head, an oddity in itself considering she had a good relationship with the mental health professionals in Edgewater Bay and it would've been a fifteen-minute drive into town rather than over two hours to Nag's Head.

It makes me wonder if she's planning on stopping at Arcania again and I'm nervous. Then again, even if she speaks to Spencer, why would he mention hiring someone to help pack the place up, let alone my name?

Besides, it wouldn't be the worst thing in the world if he broke the news about my employment to her. Saves me the initial chewing out I'll get.

Who am I kidding? It doesn't matter who tells Gran or when she learns about my new job. She's going to freak out.

When I reach the heart of town, I visit the library first. As expected, there are no updates on my DNA results. I'm disappointed, but I know not to get my hopes up, that even when they come through it doesn't mean I'll get any hits on the ancestry website. For that to happen, other members of my family, no matter how distant, need to upload their DNA too, and what are the chances of that?

If Dad has run from something traumatic in his past, would his family want to be found? Doubtful, and I need to lower my expectations that after all this, nothing may happen.

While I may never learn anything about my paternal family or get information that may lead to Dad recovering his memory, I may learn something about Mom's family and that's what I'm hoping for. I want to know everything about her so that when we meet—I'm trying to stay positive that it will happen—I'll feel a little closer to her.

Until then, I have someone who knows a lot more about my mother than I do and I'm thankful for that.

Freda lives in a tiny cottage near the wharf, where her fisherman husband works. I know where she'll be, cleaning up after the lunchtime rush when her food truck is busiest. She serves mouthwatering fish and chips, the best for miles around, and locals and tourists flock from Monday to Friday. She reserves the weekends for her family despite the badgering from hungry townsfolk who'd love her to operate the food truck twenty-four-seven.

Freda and Mel have been like aunts to me growing up. I sometimes think they're the only two Gran trusts, because she's different around them: more open, less wary, like she is around most people. It's to be expected, I guess, as she's known them the longest. I've heard them recount how Gran let them stay at The Haven when she first came to town, how they lived there for years, how she helped them financially. I've always been in awe of my grandmother's generosity and her compassion for others. I want to emulate her.

She hasn't pushed me regarding my future. I get the feeling if she had her way I'll be tethered to her apron strings forever. Being wealthy cushions us so without going to college, I'll always have a secure future. I'm hoping she feels the same way when she learns I want to spread my wings, find Mom, and experience life beyond The Haven.

The food truck is closed when I arrive, and Freda is locking up. She's wearing a cerulean polo over white jeans, her work uniform. She says the brightness of her top channels the Atlantic on a perfect summer's day. For me, I like its cheeriness. Despite her age, close to Gran's fifty-six, she wears her graying hair in two braids, the ends tied with turquoise elastics. She eschews makeup, bar a coral lipstick I've seen her wear forever.

When she catches sight of me, her face lights up and she waves me over.

"What are you doing here?"

"I came to visit you." I wrap my arms around her and her hug is as fierce as ever. "Got any leftovers?"

She chortles when we release each other. "You came for food, not to see me."

I press my hands to my chest and feign innocence. "Would I do that?"

"Yes," she says, and we laugh.

"Actually, I was hoping we could talk?"

She must catch the hint of vulnerability in my tone, because her nod is brusque. "Want to have coffee on the wharf or come to the cottage?"

"The wharf is fine." It's twenty feet away and almost deserted. Perfect. "Though I don't need a cup of coffee. Can I get you one?"

She shakes her head. "I'm good."

We fall into step together and she asks, "How's Leah? And John?"

"Good."

My response is rote because I'm not sure what's going through Gran's head these days, and I'm more than worried that Dad may be recovering his memory.

"Actually, I want to talk about Mom."

Freda stiffens as we reach a whitewashed wooden bench and sit. "I've been wondering when this day would come."

"If you know her, why haven't you said anything?"

"Because she asked me not to." She shrugs. "She wanted it to be your decision, if you wanted to know more about her or not."

"So, you're in contact now?"

I can't read the expression in her eyes. It borders on fear. "Not recently."

"When's the last time you heard from her?"

"Before your eighteenth birthday." She pauses. "I take it you have her letters and that's why you want to know more?"

I nod, the sudden lump in my throat making speaking

difficult. I know why I'm emotional. I don't just want to know more. I want to know everything. I want to know if I can trust my mother, if what she's said in her letters is true, if I'm setting myself up for a fall if I try to reach out to her now.

So many questions that Freda probably can't answer, but I must try.

"What do you want to know?"

"When you say you've kept in touch, do you see her in person or via phone or email?"

"Usually email. She asks about you." Freda hesitates, her fingers plucking at the hem of her polo top as a worry line grooves her brow. "But I have seen her once."

Her reticence worries me, like she has something to hide. "When?"

She eyeballs me. "Look, this could be nothing, so I don't want you overreacting, but I saw her in town outside the lawyer's office, and she was with your grandmother."

"What?"

"It looked like they were arguing, and Leah was trying to wrestle a letter out of your mother's hands,"

My eyebrows rise. "One of the letters for me?"

"Could be." She grimaces. "Neither of them looked happy, so I didn't intervene. I thought Robyn might pop in and see me after she dropped the letter with the lawyer, but she didn't." Freda gnaws at her bottom lip, and the furrows on her forehead deepen. "I haven't heard from her since, despite me reaching out."

I don't have a letter for my eighteenth. It wasn't in the bundle the lawyer gave me. It had seemed odd at the time, but now, after Freda's revelation, it takes on an ominous slant.

"You think Gran did something to her?"

"Don't be ridiculous," Freda snaps. "Leah wouldn't hurt anybody."

"Then what do you think happened?"

Freda's gaze slides away, but not before I glimpse guilt, which means she knows more than she's telling me.

"Your mother wanted to tell you this herself, but in light of what I've just told you, I think it's right you know." Freda inhales and blows out a breath before continuing. "Leah blackmailed her into leaving you when she had a PI dig into Robyn's past. She discovered Robyn got pregnant at sixteen and gave up the child for adoption."

Excitement tempers my shock. I have a sibling. Now, more than ever, I want those DNA results.

"When I saw them arguing, I assumed Robyn wanted to be part of your life again now you're older and perhaps Leah was blackmailing her again?" Freda shrugs. "Who knows? I can't exactly ask Leah about it, and your mother isn't answering my calls."

I press my fingers to my temples, willing away the headache that's developing. "Can you help me with something?"

"Anything." She reaches out and squeezes my hand. "I'm always here for you."

"In that case, I'm going to give you my user name and password for an ancestry site where I've submitted my DNA in the hope of finding relatives."

Freda's eyes widen in surprise, but she doesn't interrupt.

"I've been going to the library to check the results because I don't want Gran going through the search history at home, even if I wipe it, because I know she'll freak."

I don't add 'you know what she's like' because after

what Freda just told me, she knows Gran better than anybody.

"Do you mind logging in daily and checking the site for me, and calling if there's an update?"

"Of course," Freda says, her gaze filled with compassion. "But you know those ancestry sites are a long shot, right? Whoever you're trying to find needs to upload their DNA, too."

"I know, but I have to try. Especially after what you just told me."

Freda squeezes my shoulder. "It's a lot to take in. Are you okay?"

"I'm fine."

At least, I will be.

The sooner I get answers to the many questions swirling through my head, the better.

CHAPTER
FORTY

NOW

The months give way to years, and John doesn't recover his memory.

He's thoughtful and empathic and joins me in taking care of those who walk through the open doors of The Haven. We make a good team.

I'm supportive when he tells me his girlfriend, Robyn, is pregnant. I encourage them to take parenting classes. I support their decision for a home birth. I set up the room next to his as a nursery. And I hold him close the night he breaks down in tears, ten days after his precious daughter Rylee is born, as he reveals between sobs that Robyn has left and isn't coming back.

My heart breaks for my boy—he's been mine since the day he stumbled into The Haven—but I'm secretly glad. Narcissistic Robyn didn't have a maternal bone in her body and I'd known it during her entire pregnancy. Now, I have a chance to raise a baby, a chance that had been robbed from me so many years ago.

I thrive as a mother. Grandmother, technically, but in my heart Rylee is the baby I never had. I love every inch of her, from her cute little toes to the blonde fuzz on her head. I'm the one who gets up at night to feed her formula. I burp her and bathe her and rock her to sleep. John is eternally grateful, and while he loves his daughter, my heart breaks when I see that vacant glaze in his eyes sometimes, as if he can't remember how he got here and doesn't know how he'll cope.

I encourage John to take Rylee into town for her check-ups, but he hates to move far from The Haven. It's his safe place. I understand his reticence, considering he can't remember a single thing from his past, but I hoped that having Rylee might give him a new lease on life.

Instead, I'm the one who takes Rylee into Edgewater Bay regularly. I'm the one who teaches her to read, who scours online for the best homeschooling program, who takes her shopping for her first bra.

I can't believe how fast the time flies and the thought of Rylee leaving makes my heart ache. She hasn't confided in me regarding her plans. She's not keen on college and I haven't badgered her. I know it's wrong to want to keep her tethered to me, but I don't care. John and Rylee are my family. They're my world. I'll do anything to protect them.

"Gran, can I talk to you about something?"

I smile as Rylee comes up behind me and slips her arms around my waist.

"Sure." I slip the oven mitts off my hands. "Though it's interesting, the only times you want to talk these days is when I've just taken cookies out of the oven."

She laughs and gives me a squeeze before releasing me. "Oatmeal with choc chip?"

I nod as she snaffles one from the tray. "Your favorite."

"You're the best." She tosses the cookie from hand to hand, trying to cool it, and my heart clenches. She's done this same thing since she was a young child, too impatient to wait, and I blink as memories unfold before my eyes like a movie.

Rylee's first Christmas, when she toppled onto her gift, a giant stuffed unicorn, and giggled. The first time she tried sushi at six and gagged. The first time she paddled in the ocean and screamed at the chill. The first time she confided in me about a crush, a boy online who helped her with math that I knew would break her heart.

So many firsts and in that moment, I've never been more thankful that John arrived at The Haven and stayed.

"What did you want to talk about?" I transfer cookies onto a wire rack to cool, chuckling when Rylee snuck another one.

"Work."

I bite back my first response, 'you don't need to, we have plenty of money', because I don't want to stifle her. She's eighteen now and has the world at her feet. I can't tether her to The Haven, no matter how much I want to.

"What are you thinking of doing?"

"There's a wellness retreat about ninety minutes from here that's advertising a position for a cleaner."

I force a smile, when the thought of my gorgeous girl doing something so menial makes me want to scream. It's not that I'm a snob. Heck, I used to clean at Arcania all the time. But I know she's destined for great things and I want her to start her life sooner rather than later.

"Is it full time?"

She shakes her head. "Casual, so I'll still have plenty of time to help here." She pauses, her grin cheeky. "If you choose to retire, that is."

Surprised, I take a cookie and sit at the table where we share our meals. "I haven't thought about it."

Rylee rolls her eyes. "Come on, Gran. Dad said you've run this place forever, so if you want to step back, we can help more."

I'm so proud I could burst. "You want to do more around here?"

"Of course." She winks. "I'm your granddaughter, after all."

Rylee knows we're not biologically related, but she's never treated me as anything other than a blood relation. It makes me love her all the more.

Because I can't deny that over the years, in the dead of the night, I lie awake thinking about what my child would have looked like, what he or she might have achieved, what we could've done together.

I hate these futile ruminations because I'm luckier than most. John is my son in every sense of the word and Rylee is my granddaughter. I should focus on the here and now, not on a bunch of what-ifs.

"What's this wellness center called?"

Rylee laughs. "Why, so you can research them online and withhold your approval until then? Because I'm going to do this regardless, Gran."

"You're too cheeky for your own good," I say with a fond smile. "So?"

"The retreat is set up for people to digitally detox, which I think is great. Imagine, no TV, no internet, no social media. Bliss."

Rylee's trying to butter me up because she knows how

much I detest media of any kind. John and I rarely watch TV, preferring to read in the evenings, and I strictly reinforced social media guidelines when Rylee got her cell and wanted to join all the apps.

"Sounds like my kind of place," I say.

"I'm glad you think so, because I've already been to Arcania for an interview, and I've got the job."

Ice trickles through my veins as one word she said echoes through my head.

Arcania.

CHAPTER
FORTY-ONE

LEAH

NOW

"Gran, are you okay?"

Rylee scoots her chair closer and slides an arm around my shoulders. "You look like you're about to faint."

I am. I can't get oxygen to my brain. I can't move. I can't do anything. Because the thought of my precious Rylee anywhere near Arcania is unfathomable.

"Don't move." Rylee stands and heads to the sink, where she fills a glass with water before returning to the table and pressing it into my hand. "Here. Drink this."

I take a tentative sip because if I have too much I'll vomit. But Rylee's watching me with concern and I force another few sips past my lips before lowering the glass to the table.

"Do you know Arcania?"

She's smart, my girl, and I can't lie. "Yes. It used to be an orchard."

That's the thing about staying off media. You don't hear much, and the only time I spend online for the last umpteen years is to research amnesia. I deliberately blocked Arcania from my mind that day Freda told me about Ava's death. I didn't want to know anything more about that vile place and its inhabitants.

Then again, if it's a wellness retreat now, maybe they've sold it and it has new owners? It's been twenty years since I worked there, stands to reason it's had a makeover.

"Why did the mention of it freak you out?"

"Because I remember the rumors," I say, keeping my voice steady with effort. "Employees regularly disappeared, so there were many tales about the place being haunted or cursed."

To my chagrin, Rylee laughs. "Haunted, like here, you mean?"

My ghoulish girl loved when I mentioned the history of The Haven in her teens when she'd questioned me about witches inhabiting the area centuries ago—like me, history fascinated her. She sleeps heavily so never hears the nocturnal activities of our friendly ghostly inhabitants.

"Who knows?" I shrug, feigning nonchalance. "But all those people disappearing from Arcania gave it a bad reputation. I'm sure that's in the past now. Who's the owner?"

"A woman named Lucy Phillips interviewed me."

I stifle a sigh of relief. Arcania is in new hands, setting the past to rest hopefully. "What's she like?"

"Nice. Though she's selling the place, that's why she needs cleaners to get it up to scratch. Apparently, the owner, Cora Medville, died and Lucy inherited Arcania."

Shock makes me sit up straighter. After I left Arcania,

did Cora and Spencer get together and have another child?

"How old is she?"

Rylee screws up her nose when she thinks. It's cute. "Mid-twenties, maybe?"

I'd left Arcania twenty years ago, so if Rylee has misjudged Lucy's age, it's entirely possible she's Cora and Spencer's child. I know I convinced myself the two of them deserved each other when I turned my back on them, but the thought of them in a relationship still hurts.

"How did Cora die?"

"Drowned, apparently."

And just like that, I'm catapulted back to that night in the dinghy when I witnessed Spencer drowning another hapless victim.

Did Cora cross him somehow and history repeated itself?

"They found her body washed up on the beach, no signs of foul play. I looked it up because I wanted to make sure nothing weird happened. I wouldn't want to work at a place like that if it had." Rylee's head cocks to one side as she studies me. "You're asking a lot of questions, Gran. You really don't like that place, huh?"

"No, I don't."

I want to tell her to steer clear, but I know my granddaughter. Warning her off will only make her want to work at Arcania more. She's headstrong, just like me.

"Well, you shouldn't worry. An older guy interviewed me too. Said he'd worked there for over forty years."

For the second time in as many minutes, my blood runs cold.

"Spencer Hadley. He's moving away once the place is sold. Said he'd be helping get it ship shape alongside the staff Lucy hires."

I freeze like I've been dunked in the Atlantic on a winter's day.

Rylee will be working with Spencer.

My granddaughter and the man I thought I knew, but didn't know at all.

The man who's dangerous.

I can't let that happen.

"Rylee, I don't want you working there."

I want to forbid her, to lock her here and throw away the key.

Predictably, she bristles. "With all due respect, Gran, I'm old enough to make my own decisions." She stands, but ducks down to press a kiss to my cheek. "I start next week."

As I watch Rylee grab two more cookies on her way out, my mind is whirring. I don't trust Spencer, and if he finds out Rylee is my granddaughter...what is he capable of?

An outlandish idea pops into my head. It's crazy, but doable.

If I buy Arcania now, before Rylee has a chance to work there, she won't cross paths with Spencer again. Because a small part of me can't help but think that maybe he already knows Rylee is my granddaughter and this is his way of toying with me?

For what motivation, I don't know, and maybe I'm imagining the worst when there's no need.

Regardless, I need to get Spencer out of our lives once and for all.

Buying Arcania will guarantee it.

Because once I confront Spencer, he'll be under no illusions who holds the power.

I'm going to tell him.

Everything.

FORTY-TWO

RYLEE

NOW

I want to tell Dad about Gran forbidding me to work at Arcania. But first, I'm going to finish reading Mom's letters. After what Freda told me—witnessing Gran and Mom tussling before my eighteenth—I have to see if there's anything in her letters that I can use to confront Gran with.

I'm torn. Between loyalty to my grandmother who's raised me, loved me, and given me everything I could possibly want, and a mother who abandoned me but I'd give anything to know.

I sit on the floor next to my bed and slide the box from its hiding place. When I pick up the bundle of letters, I lift them to my nose as usual and sniff. Crazy, I know, as they've been at the lawyer's office forever, and all I smell is the faintest blend of ink and musty paper, but I do it every time I read these letters because I harbor an irrational hope I'll smell Mom.

The remaining letters are much the same: updates on her job, her life, ending with a reinforcement of how much she loves and misses me. But it's the letter for my seventeenth birthday I'm most interested in. Because if Mom had planned to visit for my eighteenth and give me a letter in person, I want to see if there's a hint.

And if Gran's been keeping tabs on her all these years.

There's no other explanation for how they would've been arguing in town unless Gran knew Mom had planned on coming back, because I refuse to believe in coincidence that Gran saw Mom and accidentally ran into her.

Hopefully, this letter will give me some clue.

Dear Rylee,

Happy seventeenth, darling girl. I can't believe that in one year, I'll get to see you. It will be the longest three hundred and sixty-five days of my life, but I've been this patient, I have to keep the faith.

Why will I see you? Because when I left you, I was always coming back. Your grandmother knew this. I told her that when you turned eighteen, I would return and let you decide for yourself if you wanted me in your life or not. It's what has kept me going all these years, the thought of being reunited with you.

I understand you may not want to have anything to do with me, but I'll face that possibility when it happens. Know that I won't hold it against you if that's what you decide, because you're my daughter and I'll do anything for you to be happy.

So here's my plan. Rather than posting my annual letter, I'm going to bring it in person. But it won't be my usual letter. I'm not sending it to Barry Mackay. I'm giving it to Freda to pass on to you. And it won't be a letter. It will be a time and place for us to meet, along with the charm bracelet I promised you. The note will also advise you to go to the lawyer's and read all my previous letters before we meet. That way, you'll have an idea of where I'm coming from and hopefully, smooth the way to a reunion.

The decision will be entirely yours and know that I'll understand if you don't want to see me. It won't change my love for you. Or the hope that one day we'll be reunited.

So if you've read this far, hopefully we'll be meeting one day soon.

I love you, now and always.
Mom xx

MY CHEEKS ARE damp by the time I finish and I slide the letter back into its envelope.

If I'd received her last letter with details of when and where to meet, nothing would've stopped me from doing just that.

But Gran stopped it.

She somehow convinced Mom to walk away from me a second time and I don't think I can forgive her for it.

I'm not sure how much of this to share with my father, but I'm worried about Gran's increasingly bizarre behavior and he's the only one I can turn to.

When I go downstairs, he's in the kitchen, rubbing a spice mix into a piece of brisket. His face is serene, as it always is when he's prepping food or cooking. The kitchen is definitely his happy place and, not for the first time, I wonder if he'd been a chef in his pre-amnesiac days and muscle memory tethered him to food.

"Hey, Dad, got a minute?"

He glances up from the slab of meat and blinks, like he's been far away. "Sure, Lee. I'll pop this in the fridge to marinate first."

I slide onto a stool at the island and wait, knowing he'll clean up before we talk. Another giveaway he might've been a chef: he likes a pristine kitchen and will always clear up after he's been prepping food.

Once he's slid the meat into the fridge, put away the spices, wiped down the countertop, and washed his hands, he sits on the stool next to me. "What's up, Lee? You look like something's on your mind."

I want to tell him everything.

About Freda revealing Mom had given a child up for adoption years before she'd had me, how Gran had blackmailed her into leaving because of it, how Freda saw them fighting only a few months ago, about the letters, all of it.

But I don't want to bombard him with too much information at once, and I don't know how he'll react to hearing all that stuff about Mom. So I settle for telling him what he can control.

Gran.

"You know how Gran's been acting weird lately?"

He nods, pensive. "Yeah. I'm a tad worried, too."

"Well, I mentioned I got a part-time job at Arcania, and she freaked out. Forbid me to take it."

I watch him closely to see if the mention of Arcania makes him queasy again, but apart from a slight paling, he's okay.

"She forbade you?"

I nod. "It's not rational. Can we talk to her together? Get her to see reason? Because I really want to work there."

His expression softens. "It'll be your first job. Of course you should do it."

"So you'll talk to her with me?"

"Absolutely." He hesitates, and the frown between his brows returns. "But first, I want to see this Arcania for myself."

I should protest, particularly after his reaction the first time I mentioned it. But I'm curious. What if Gran's not the only one with links to Arcania and Dad just doesn't know it?

"I have a strong feeling here." Dad presses a hand to his gut. "That I need to see this place for myself."

I hesitate a fraction longer before nodding. "Okay. Let's go."

CHAPTER
FORTY-THREE

LEAH

NOW

T he realtor is running thirty minutes late—car trouble, according to her text—but it doesn't matter.

I know my way around Arcania.

It appears deserted when I park in my old spot near the corner of the mansion, beside the path that leads to the ocean. The feeling of coming home is surreal as I get out of my car and glance at the familiar French provincial lines of the house: the many windows, the new paint job.

This place was never my home.

I follow the path to the back, intrigued by the renovations that have taken place. While the front facade has maintained Arcania's historical roots, the back has been modernized, with a large glass enclosed studio filled with yoga mats added onto an offshoot of the kitchen, and a huge dining room with a table that looks like it could seat forty. A pretty gazebo has been built at the edge of the old orchard, the perfect spot for meditating in the outdoors.

So it's true. Arcania is now a wellness retreat. I researched it online when Rylee first mentioned it and it looked too good to be true, so I had to see for myself.

It's baffling, how a place that harbors so much darkness from the past is a welcoming refuge for those needing to detox. False advertising at its finest. Then again, apart from the rumors about the workers that disappeared, nobody knows the truth about Cora and Spencer but me. And with Cora gone, that only leaves one man to confront.

Because deep down, that's why I'm here. Rylee mentioned that once Arcania sells, Spencer is moving away. He'll get away with one murder—maybe two if my suspicions he got rid of Cora too are correct—and I can't let that happen.

My love for Spencer has turned to hate over the years.

I've told no-one about how much he meant to me, how I stuck around in this gothic hellhole for nineteen years because of him. I know that's on me, and it makes me sound pathetic, but the heart wants what the heart wants.

But turns out, keeping secrets isn't healthy. My resentment toward Spencer has festered over the years and grown to monstrous proportions.

He doesn't deserve to escape scot-free.

Revealing the truth of what I saw that day at the cove two decades ago to the police will be more laughable now than it would've been then. Which only leaves one option.

I need to take care of business myself.

As if thoughts of the man conjure him up, I see Spencer walking toward me. He's wearing a wetsuit and has diving equipment slung over his shoulder.

I hate that my heart gives a betraying lurch. Even in his

sixties, he's still attractive: his caramel curls are almost white, and the lines of time groove his face, but he's lean and fit, with the easy lope of a man comfortable in his own skin.

Why wouldn't he be, considering he thinks he got away with murder?

I see the exact moment he catches sight of me. He stumbles and the wind whips away the curse I lipread.

I can't move. I want to walk toward him, but fear roots my feet to the spot. It's nice in theory, thinking I'll confront him, but what do I expect to get out of this other than some petty revenge?

He strides toward me, his expression a mix of joy and wariness. I hate that he's happy to see me. Why couldn't he look at me like that back when I wanted him too, when I would've given anything to be the woman who captured his heart rather than Cora?

"Leah. It's been too long." He lowers the diving equipment to his feet and steps forward to envelop me in a hug.

I stiffen, but this is Spencer, the man I loved for too long, and I relax into the embrace, pressing my cheek to his, savoring his stubble scraping my skin. He smells the same, a heady blend of the ocean and the citrus-scented soap he favored, and I hate the leap of my traitorous heart.

He releases me too soon and steps back until we're at arm's length apart. "You look amazing," he says, his lopsided smile as familiar as his scent, and I grit my teeth against the urge to bury myself into his arms again.

"Thanks."

I dressed carefully for this confrontation today. Black pencil skirt, fitted pinstriped jacket, white silk shell top, patent heels. Not from vanity, but from necessity. I need to present a confident front, like donning armor before going into battle.

"What are you doing here after all this time?"

"I heard Arcania's on the market and wanted to see it for myself."

"Why? You thinking of buying it?" He laughs at what he thinks is a joke and it snaps me out of my sentimental fog.

This man doesn't care about me. He never did. He knows nothing about me—where I live, my financial situation, if I have family—because he never asked. It will be gratifying to wipe the smirk off his face.

"Actually, yes, that's why I'm here. The realtor's running late, so I thought I'd look around, check out the changes."

I stifle a laugh at his open-mouth shock.

"Did you win the lottery?" Suspicion darkens the hazel eyes I once could've drowned in.

I shake my head. "I've always had a trust fund. One benefit of having guilt-ridden parents who'd do anything to keep their precious reputation intact once threatened by their daughter."

Respect replaces the suspicion in his eyes. "Good for you." He gestures to the mansion behind me. "And I'm glad you're buying this place. If anyone should have it, it should be someone who knows it."

"And all its secrets," I say, throwing it out there casually, not missing the tightening around his mouth. "I was sorry to hear about Ava, and more recently, Cora. Death seems to be entrenched here."

He pales slightly. "Yet you're buying it."

"I live with ghosts every day."

"What does that mean?"

I have no intention of telling him where I live—and

Rylee, who I'll protect at all costs—so I shrug. "My house is haunted. It doesn't bother me."

I deliberately widen my eyes in false innocence. "Not like this place, though. Imagine if the ghosts could talk." My laugh is brittle, and he's staring at me like a wrangler eyes a skittish colt. "Cora drowned, huh?"

And there it is, Spencer's tell. The flexing of his fingers and the bulging of a vein at his right temple. I'd seen it the day after he disappeared with Cora in the orchard, and the day after what he did to Sam and I questioned him. Some things never change.

"Yes. I found her washed up on the beach…" he trails off, genuine sorrow making the corners of his mouth droop. "She didn't deserve to die that way."

"Nobody deserves to die," I snap, regretting my outburst when his gaze locks on mine and the suspicion is back.

He stares at me for what seems like an eternity before he finally says, "Why are you really here, Leah?"

He's always been astute, and I need to give him some semblance of the truth, because the last thing I want is for him to discover my link to Rylee.

"I'm here because if I'm buying this place, I want a clean slate. No more secrets, no more bodies."

He flinches, realizing he's given away too much without saying a word.

"What really happened to Sam? Did you need him out of the way so Ava wouldn't be tied to Arcania?"

Shock renders him mute, so I continue. "It must've broken your heart when she died a month after Sam disappeared. So whatever you did to Sam was for nothing." I twist the knife a little harder. "Must be unbearable, living with that kind of guilt."

He gives a little shake, as if coming out of a stupor. "You don't know what you're talking about. Ava didn't die…"

It's my turn to gape as he continues, "At least, not here. Not then."

I recover my wits enough to ask, "What are you saying?"

"Ava was pregnant, so I helped fake her death so she could escape here and raise her child in a better environment."

"You faked her death?" I sound like an idiot repeating what he's just said, but I can't help it. Of all the scenarios I'd envisaged, this isn't one of them.

He nods, his expression bleak. "We always shared a special bond. Deep down, I knew I was her father, even if Cora lied to me about that. Lucy is her child and after Cora's death, we did a DNA test. Turns out, Ava was mine."

"So you have a granddaughter?"

"Yes." His expression softens, the way it used to whenever Cora was around. "She's incredible. I'm moving to Manhattan to be closer to her once Arcania sells."

I take no pleasure in my supposition that Cora lied to him and her baby was Spencer's was correct. But it irks that the man who robbed his own daughter of happiness by murdering her boyfriend now gets to live happily ever after with his own flesh and blood.

"What happened to Ava?"

"She fled to Manhattan, had Lucy, led a quiet life off the grid. Cora found out recently and we think she pushed Ava in front of a bus deliberately."

"What the—"

"I know, it's horrific. She had some twisted plan to groom Lucy to take over here, so we think that was her motivation for getting rid of Ava." Sadness contorts his face before he scrubs a hand over it. "It's over now. And I can't wait to get away from this place."

Something doesn't add up. "If you hate Arcania so much, why did you stick around after you helped Ava escape?"

"How do you know I stayed?"

I can't say that Rylee told me she'd heard he'd been here for forty years when he interviewed her, so I say, "You're here, aren't you?"

Thankfully, he buys my response. "I stayed in case Ava's child ever returned and, as it turns out, she did. She saw the *vegvisir* tattoo on Ava's foot after she died, researched it, and discovered the link to Arcania. Lucy came and stayed here as a guest, trying to discover her mother's links to this place. Then Cora died, and we discovered Lucy had inherited Arcania."

"You're not bitter, that Cora didn't leave the place to you?"

He snorts. "Why would she? I was nothing but the stooge she duped for years. I obviously meant little to her." He gestures at the mansion. "Do you want to come inside and look around before the realtor gets here?"

"Sure. Just let me grab something from my car."

"No worries. I'm going diving soon, so I'll get my stuff ready while I wait for you." He unlocks the side door and as I get a glimpse inside, it's like being catapulted back in time.

It makes me question, what am I really doing here?

CHAPTER

FORTY-FOUR

RYLEE

NOW

Arcania's driveway is long and as I pull up outside the house and catch sight of Gran's car, I freeze.

Dad sees it at the same time I do, and his confused gaze flies to mine. "What's she doing here?"

"I guess we're about to find out."

I'm glad Gran is here. It means she can't lie to us anymore. She'll have to come clean.

I'm about to step from the car when I hear a sharp intake of breath, followed by a long exhale akin to a groan. I glance at Dad and he's pale, his skin a deathly gray that makes me wonder if I'm doing the wrong thing, prompting his memory like this.

"Dad?"

He doesn't respond, his gaze catatonic, riveted to the mansion. His breathing becomes shallow, choppy, as his fingers pluck at the stiff denim of his jeans.

Hell.

I put the car into reverse, desperate to get out of here. In my quest for answers, I've done this to my poor, sweet dad and I'll never forgive myself.

"Stop," he says, barely above a croak, and I hesitate, torn between wanting to floor it out of here and hope that I haven't caused irreversible damage, and wanting to hear what my father has to say.

"I'll be okay," he adds, his tone stronger as he lays a hand on my arm. His palm's clammy, but when I glance at him, he's regained color and isn't looking so shell-shocked. "Park the car and we'll get out."

"You sure?"

He nods, determination in his eyes. "I'm sure."

I turn off the engine, my hands trembling slightly as I step from the car. Dad hesitates a moment before getting out too and as our gazes lock, I'm relieved to see he's lost the haunted look from a few moments ago.

His gaze drifts toward the house again, and I see him flinch.

"You remember being here, don't you?"

He nods, his fingers curling into fists he thrusts into his pockets. "The minute I laid eyes on the mansion, I knew I've been here before and it wasn't good."

I hate to ask the next question, but I have to. "Do you think Arcania has something to do with your memory loss?"

He shrugs. "I don't know. But it gives me chills knowing I've been here before, and whatever happened can't be good."

I hate the thought of causing Dad unnecessary pain, but I figure the faster we look around, the easier it'll be because then we can leave ASAP.

"Do you remember anything?" I point to the house. "Shall we take a tour, see if anything jogs your memory?"

His expression is wary as he nods. However, we barely make it to the corner of the house before Gran comes around from the back. Her mouth drops open in shock when she sees us, and before I can say anything, she comes flying at us like a crazy person, flapping her arms, waving us away.

"You can't be here," she yells, her eyes wide as she darts a frantic glance over her shoulder. "You have to leave."

"Calm down, Gran. We're just—"

"Go. Now." She grabs our arms and starts dragging us toward the car.

Dad and I baulk at the same time.

"Honey, go wait in the car while I talk to your grandmother," Dad says, his tone resolute.

I don't want to leave him alone with her ire because this is all my fault, but he adds, "Please. It'll be okay."

Gran releases me and I surreptitiously rub my arm where her fingers dug in. "We'll talk later, young lady."

Translated: she'll give me a tongue lashing I'll never forget.

I don't care. All this subterfuge must end.

Now.

FORTY-FIVE

LEAH

NOW

I can't breathe.

Years of secrets are pressing my lungs, restricting my air flow, and spots dance before my eyes.

But I can't pass out. Because I need to get John out of here before he discovers the truth.

I can't fathom what might happen if he remembers. He means too much to me, the son I never had, and I can't bear the thought of him being in pain. And that's exactly what's going to happen if his memory returns.

"Leah, stop." He lays a hand on my arm and only then do I realize I've been practically jogging along the path that leads to the beach, away from the house.

"John, you can't be here." I stifle a sob as our eyes meet, and I see a flicker of awareness.

He remembers.

"I'm okay," he says, though the slightest quiver in his voice undermines his statement. "But we need to talk."

I nod. "We do. But not here." I hesitate, not wanting to know the truth but needing to be forearmed for what's coming. "Are you having flashbacks?"

He grimaces. "Not really. But every time Rylee has mentioned Arcania I feel funny, which is why I demanded she bring me here so I can see for myself." He scrubs a hand over his face and it's trembling. "The moment I caught sight of the mansion, I knew I've been here before. I felt sick." He presses a hand to his stomach. "In here."

He's not the only one. Nausea churns in my gut as I realize this incredible, sweet man will now learn the truth.

I know my fear is irrational because I've withheld the truth all these years for his own good. I've been nothing but loving and nurturing, so I hope he won't resent me. But if anyone knows the dangers of old secrets resurfacing, it's me.

That's why I have to silence Spencer once and for all.

If John hears the truth, it's going to be from me. My version of the truth, that is.

"Do you trust me?" I clasp his hand and squeeze it tight, hoping to convey a strength I don't feel.

"Of course." He squeezes back. "You've been like a mother all these years."

"Then go home. I promise I won't be far behind you, and when I get there, we'll talk."

He studies my face, his scrutiny unnerving. "You know about what happened to me here, don't you?"

I settle for a partial truth. "A little."

His shoulders square and his jaw clenches. "Then it's more than I do, and I need to hear it."

Relief filters through me. Everything will be okay. I'm still in control of the situation.

"There's someone I need to say goodbye to inside the house, so I'll do that and I won't be far behind you and Rylee."

Thankfully, he nods and releases my hand. "See you at home."

I wait until he rounds the corner of the house on his way to the front car park before sprinting to the mansion. I'd been on tenterhooks the entire time I was talking to John, willing Spencer not to come outside. Now, I need to keep him busy, give Rylee and John a few minutes to leave.

I see more of Spencer's diving equipment propped against the veranda, which means he must've come out at some point. Had he seen us? I can't have him going out the front, so I burst through the back door, memories of the past assailing me. Daphne in the kitchen, whipping up the nachos the orchard workers loved so much. Cora sitting at the table, menu planning for the week ahead. Spencer sneaking peanut butter cookies before they cooled.

I blink rapidly, surprised by the sting of tears. I can't afford to get melancholic, not when I have a job to do.

Get Spencer to admit the truth, then ensure he stays away from my family.

"Spencer?" I call out as I enter the foyer, trepidation tiptoeing down my spine when he doesn't answer. "You in here?"

"I'm upstairs. Be down in a sec."

I sag against the island in relief. If he's upstairs, he's nowhere near the parking lot. But my relief is short-lived. What if he looks out a window, sees Rylee's car, and is curious why she's here? I assume he saw her car when he interviewed her for the job, so hopefully, even if he sees her car, he'll think she's here to scope out the place before she starts.

I hear Spencer's heavy tread descend the stairs, much slower than when he'd been a young man. We're older now and I wonder if dredging up the past is worth it.

Then I remember what he did and I'm angry all over again.

He can't get away with it.

When he reaches the bottom of the staircase, I'm glaring at him, my arms folded, my chin jutting. I'm spoiling for a fight.

He knows it too because he takes a minuscule step backward, like he expects I'll strike him. "What's going on?"

"I want you to tell me the truth."

His right eyebrow rises a fraction at my combative tone. "About?"

"Sam."

He stiffens, instantly on guard. "You're obsessed about this. Let it go—"

"I saw you." I pause for emphasis. "I saw you kill him."

Spencer blanches and staggers back. "You're out of your mind."

"Am I?"

I snicker, wishing I could savor this moment of victory, but feeling hollow instead. I thought it would feel good, confronting the man I'd once loved, getting him to confess. But he looks old, like he's shrunk in on himself, and I feel nothing but pity.

"I used to watch you at the cove," I say. "Did you know I was crazy about you?"

To his credit, he doesn't lie about this. "Yes, I knew."

The corners of his mouth curve into a smug smirk, and

my palm itches to slap him. "I knew you were there that day, spying on me as usual. I had no intention of killing Sam. I just wanted to scare him."

"Scare him into leaving Arcania?"

"Precisely. As long as he was around, Ava would never leave." He shrugs. "With him out of the picture, I could save my daughter."

He's so nonchalant while I'm trembling with rage. "So you were happy to sacrifice one life for another?"

"Ava was my priority."

"And how did that work out for you?"

It's a low blow I'm not proud of and he flinches.

"She lived a decent life far from here and raised her daughter safe from Cora's clutches. That's all I ever wanted."

I see glimpses of a broken man, but he's not cowering as I expected when he admitted what he'd done to Sam. "Want to know what I want?"

"What?"

"To buy this place and burn it to the ground."

He gasps, his skin a sickly gray. "You wouldn't."

"Why do you care?"

"Because Arcania is special. Don't you feel it?"

He's barely speaking above a whisper and when there's silence, the hair on my arms snaps to attention as the faintest caress brushes the nape of my neck. There's nothing there, of course, and I don't turn around. I'm used to ancient houses and their ghosts.

"Considering the number of deaths here, I would think the ghosts would appreciate it being demolished."

He shudders, his eyes fixed at some point over my shoulder. "Too many deaths..."

"When are you leaving?"

"Tomorrow. Lucy has hired a girl who lives in Edgewater Bay to start packing rooms next week, but I don't need to be around for that."

He doesn't need to be around permanently.

I'll make sure of it.

FORTY-SIX

RYLEE

NOW

Dad and I are prepping leftover pot roast when Gran walks into the kitchen, arriving at The Haven about twenty minutes after us. She's pale, but there's determination in her eyes. Dad told me on the drive back that Gran wants to talk about Arcania with him and I'm busting with curiosity.

If she thinks I will not be privy to that conversation, she's dreaming.

"You're both okay?" She asks as a way of greeting and I refrain from rolling my eyes. Whatever her connection to Arcania beyond working there decades ago, the place isn't as spooky as she makes out.

"We're fine," I say, and Dad nods.

We spoke little on the way home and I didn't push him. If his memories are coming back, better that happens gradually.

"Are you hungry?" I gesture at the countertop. "We're making sandwiches."

"I'm not hungry," she says, then does something so out of character that Dad and me gape.

Gran opens the cupboard above the stove where we keep brandy for cooking, pours herself a generous slosh, and downs the lot in a few gulps.

"I needed that," she murmurs, rinsing her glass and placing it on the sideboard like it's the most natural things in the world for her to ingest a large amount of alcohol in one go.

When she catches us staring at her in open-mouth shock, she laughs. "What? I needed that after being back at Arcania today." She jabs a finger at us. "And to cope with the shock of seeing both of you there."

Thankful she's brought up the topic, I'm about to ask what her deal with Arcania is when my cell vibrates in my jacket pocket. I slide it out and one glance at the screen has my heart pounding.

Freda.

"I have to take this," I say, injecting as much noncha-lance as I can muster into my voice and failing miserably by Gran's narrow-eyed stare. "Be back in a moment."

I take the stairs two at a time, desperate for the sanctity of my room, when I answer.

"Hey, Freda. Do you have news?"

She chuckles. "Hello to you too, young lady."

I'm about to apologize for my rudeness when she says, "Yes, I have news. When I logged onto your ancestry account today, there'd been an update."

I'm lightheaded for a moment and sag against the back of my bedroom door. "Do I have family?"

"Yes. There was a match." She pauses and I hear a sharp intake of breath before she continues. "A close match."

My hand's shaking as I press the cell to my ear. "Tell me."

"You have a sister."

Tears fill my eyes, and my throat constricts.

I have a sister. My own flesh and blood.

It must be the child Mom gave up for adoption years before she had me. If only I'd known about her existence earlier, I could've got to know her sooner. Gran knew, but I understand why she kept it from me. Her overprotective-ness knows no bounds and if she went as far as black-mailing Mom to leave me, no way in hell she'd tell me about a half-sibling.

An overwhelming mix of sadness, regret, and anger make my legs shake and I slide down the door until my butt hits the floor.

"Does she have a name?"

"Uh-huh."

When Freda reveals who my sister is, the room spins, and I drop the phone.

What the...?

FORTY-SEVEN

LEAH

NOW

Rylee is pale when she returns to the kitchen and I want to ask who she'd been speaking to on the phone. But there are more pressing matters.

Namely, telling the people I love the most in the world the semi-truth.

I wait for Rylee to sit beside her father before I begin.

"I need to tell you both something and perhaps it's best if you wait until I finish before asking questions," I say, managing to keep my voice steady when inside, I feel like screaming.

"Okay," John says, while Rylee merely nods, appearing shellshocked. I want to ask her what's wrong so badly, but it'll have to wait.

"I lied to you both when you first asked me about Arcania. I did know it." I pause, thinking 'here goes nothing'. "I used to work there."

John and Rylee wear identical expressions of shock, and I hurry on. "I didn't need to work when I first arrived here because I had money, as you know. But the mansion intrigued me and I developed a crush on an employee there, so I started working there. I didn't tell anyone there my personal business, so they didn't know I was wealthy."

Heat creeps into my cheeks. "I thought if anyone knew, it would jeopardize my chances with the man I loved. So I kept to myself. I worked hard. And I fell harder for him."

"How long did you work there?" John asks.

"Almost twenty years."

They're open-mouthed again and I need to be careful how I proceed, giving them just enough information without revealing too much.

"I know it sounds crazy, working that long when I didn't have to, but I loved this man and would've done anything for him."

"Including waste two decades of your life apparently," Rylee says, her dry response earning a frown from her father.

"It's not logical, I know, and I would hate if you did anything remotely similar, Rylee, but I was alone in the world after a cloistered, emotionless upbringing, and getting attention from this man became my world, my motivation for getting up in the morning."

John and Rylee stare at me with wide-eyed pity. Good. I need them to feel sorry for me and not question me too deeply.

"Over those years, employees came and went. Rumors abounded about foul play. The owners died in a boat explosion and their creepy son took over. Then he died too, fell down stairs, and I witnessed stuff I shouldn't have..." I suppress a shudder. "This is the part I hope you won't judge me for, but I did what I did to protect you, John."

Before I can reveal anything, John says, "I used to work there too, didn't I?"

I nod and Rylee mutters, "No way."

"Yes. You worked in the orchard for a few months before I left, so I recognized you instantly when I found you sitting in my living room that day you walked in here. But you didn't recognize me, so I knew you'd been through some kind of trauma. And when the doctor confirmed the dissociative amnesia, I knew something bad must've happened to you at Arcania and I wanted to protect you from all that."

"I worked there..." he says, his voice soft and tremulous. "I wish I could remember what happened."

"Maybe it's for the best you can't?" I interlock my fingers to stop from plucking nervously at the hem of my shirt. "Bad things happened at Arcania and if what you went through was awful enough to wipe your memory, I didn't want you facing any further trauma, so I made sure to sever all ties with the place."

Understanding glints in Rylee's eyes. "That's why you don't want me working there, in case it jogs Dad's memory?"

I nod. "I'm terrified. So imagine how I felt when I saw you both there earlier today." I make circles at my temples. "I went a little nuts and I'm sorry."

The man I've raised as my own son stares at me, bewilderment clouding his gaze. "So my real name is John?"

"Yes. Though I never knew your surname. We barely spoke while you worked at Arcania. So when you turned up here, I stuck with your first name but gave you my surname."

Because ever since my parents had forced me to have an

abortion, I'd always wondered what my child would've been like. Would I have had a boy like John—kind, sweet, nurturing—or a girl like Rylee—loving, strong, inquisitive?

John walking into The Haven had been the best thing to ever happen to me and I'm never going to be sorry for raising him as the son I never had.

That ridiculous scrying I'd done with Mel and Freda so many years ago had been eerily accurate. I'd seen a baby boy morph into a man, so I like to think John arriving at The Haven had been fate's way of giving me the child I craved and lost.

"I know you both must have a million questions, but for now just know that everything I did was because I love you both and I'd do it all again. Also, there's something else I have to tell you."

They remain silent, matching right eyebrows quirked in curiosity, so I continue.

"I'm buying Arcania. We've done so much good for those in need here at The Haven over the years, imagine what can be achieved with a mansion the size of Arcania."

Rylee's eyeing me with suspicion and I hope to God I've convinced them both of my intentions.

"That's a big undertaking," John says. "You'll have to hire a huge staff."

I shrug. "I know, but it's my way of giving back. Of cleansing the past from that place and replacing it with a brighter future."

I eyeball Rylee. "I'm hoping you'll help, sweetheart. You can stay here if you'd like and run this place, or start fresh at Arcania."

Rylee gapes a little. "I don't know what to say."

"Just think about it. No rush. That's what I was doing over there earlier. I was supposed to meet the realtor, but they never showed." I give a self-deprecating laugh. "Not that it matters, as I already know what the place looks like."

Did I ever.

"Anyway, I love you both and I'm sorry for lying to you, even if my reasons were to protect you."

"That's okay." John hugs me and I finally breathe a sigh of relief.

But it's short-lived because Rylee's embrace is stiff and awkward, like she knows I'm not telling the entire truth.

RYLEE

NOW

Gran's not telling the truth.

Sure, her explanation about wanting to protect Dad and I sounds true enough, but I can tell when she's being evasive. She can't quite meet my eye and she bustled Dad out into the backyard to pluck herbs like she couldn't get away from me fast enough.

What is it about Arcania that has her so jittery?

It doesn't make sense, considering she's buying the place. She's doing a good thing, wanting to convert it into another refuge for the homeless, but it all seems too trite, like she's tying up loose ends or something.

Anyway, I have more important things to worry about.

Like reaching out to my sister.

I pick up my cell, but before I can call Arcania to get the number I need, the cell vibrates in my hand. It's a cell number I don't recognize but I answer it.

"Rylee? It's Lucy Phillips."

My heart starts pounding and I clutch the cell to my ear. "Hey Lucy, I was just going to call you."

Her chuckle is nervous. "I'm guessing you got the alert from the ancestry website too?"

"Yeah."

I'm speechless, a bundle of nerves and disbelief.

Lucy Phillips is my sister, the baby Mom gave up six years before she had me.

What are the odds?

"I think we should meet," she says. "Chat about all this in person."

"I'd like that. How about you come over here?"

That way, I can confront Gran. I'm sick of hiding what I know about her and Mom. If she blackmailed my mother into leaving me because of what she discovered about Mom giving up Lucy, I want the truth to come out. No more secrets. I'm sick of them.

I also want to get to know my sister and that means Dad and Gran knowing Lucy exists and my familial bond to her.

"You're about ninety minutes from Arcania, right?"

"Yes, I can text you the address."

"That'll be great. I just arrived not that long ago to finalize a few things with Spencer, but he's gone diving, so I'll leave now."

My hand shakes as I grip the cell tighter. "Are you freaking out about this as much as I am?"

"A little." She exhales loudly. "There's been a lot of secrets in my family, so when I recently discovered Spencer is my grandfather, I sent my DNA to that website in case I had more family I didn't know about. Turns out, I do."

Spencer is her grandfather?

Does that mean he's mine too, or is he related on her paternal side?

Yet more questions I want answers to.

"I was shocked when I heard the results because we already know each other. Big coincidence, huh?"

"Sure is," she says. "Freaky."

I'm too much of a realist to believe in coincidences, and this one seems exceptionally bizarre. Lucy and I really need to talk.

"I'm looking forward to chatting in person," I say.

"Me too. I'll leave now. And Rylee?"

"Yeah?"

"I'm glad I have a sister."

I'm too choked up to say more than, "see you soon," before I hang up.

THANKFULLY, Lucy must speed the entire way from Arcania to The Haven because she arrives in seventy-five minutes rather than ninety. The moment I hear a car pull up outside, I open the front door and run down the driveway.

When she gets out of the car, I scan her face for the slightest resemblance to me, but I can't see any similarities.

"Hey," she says, one corner of her mouth curved in an awkward smile as she takes a step toward me.

"Hey," I parrot, unsure whether to hug her or pinch her to see if she's real and not some figment of my wishful imagination to find family.

"This is weird, huh?" She crossed the few feet that separate us and opens her arms.

I don't hesitate and hug her so fiercely I hear a little yelp.

"Sorry," I say, releasing her and stepping back. "I'm just so happy to see you."

"Same here."

We grin at each other and that's when I see it, something I hadn't noticed when she interviewed me. We both have a tiny mole nestled in the groove on the right side of our nose. The fact we share DNA is proof enough we're related, but seeing that mole reinforces this isn't some sick cosmic joke and it's real.

Lucy is my sister.

"Do you want to talk in the backyard?" I gesture behind me. "My grandmother and father are inside, so it'll give us some privacy."

"Sure," she says, falling into step beside me as we follow the path around the side of the house. "This place has the same vibe as Arcania, but on a smaller scale."

I hope she means gothic and not creepy. Because I've always felt safe here, whereas Arcania gives off distinct creepy vibes.

"Gran bought it many years ago and offers sanctuary to anyone who needs a place to stay."

"That's wonderful," she says, but I see her eyeing the house like she's suspicious.

I don't mention Gran's historical links to Arcania, or the fact she's buying it now. I want Lucy and me to start with a clean slate, and not complicate our relationship with Gran's connection to Arcania.

When we reach the backyard, I choose the small wrought iron table near the shed, out of sight from the house in case Gran or Dad catch sight of us and want to come meet my new friend before we've had a chance to talk. I want Lucy to myself for a little while before I introduce her to my other family.

"Do you want something to drink?"

She shakes her head. "Maybe later."

We sit and there's an awkward pause before I rush in. "I know you were adopted out, but have you had any contact with our mother? Any letters? Because she sent them yearly to me and I only just got them, so it'll be great to meet her together—"

"Rylee, that's not possible." The color drains from Lucy's face and she's staring at me in confusion. "I wasn't adopted."

"But..." I trail off as Lucy's implication sinks in. "If we don't share the same mother..."

She nods, wide-eyed, as she glances at something—or someone—over my shoulder. "We share the same father."

I turn to find Dad staring at us in open-mouthed shock.

FORTY-NINE

LEAH

NOW

Foreboding trickles down my spine as I glance out the kitchen window and see John standing still, his back so rigid his shoulders elevate. He's staring at something I can't see and when he doesn't move for a full minute, I decide to make sure he's okay.

Surely the snippets I revealed about Arcania haven't jogged his memory?

If anything, visiting Arcania in person wouldn't done that and I'd been beyond relieved he hadn't remembered the past. But what if it's a delayed reaction and memories have returned now?

My feet fly across the yard at the possibility, and I skid to a halt when I see Rylee sitting with a young woman, both staring at John in shock.

I lay a hand on John's shoulder. "Is everything alright?"

He shrugs off my hand and takes a step forward. "How can you be my daughter?"

And with those six words, my world comes crashing down.

The blood drains from my face and I sway, blindly reaching toward the nearest tree to steady myself. Bile rises in my throat and I swallow it down with effort, my heart pounding so loud it reverberates in my ears.

"Gran?" Rylee's voice sounds like it's coming from miles away as she slides an arm around my waist and leads me to a chair beside the woman.

John's first daughter.

The moment Spencer told me that Ava hadn't died in the swamp and he'd helped her fake her death so she could escape Arcania to have her baby—and that baby had inherited Arcania—I've been terrified this day would come.

I don't know how Rylee has discovered the link between her and Lucy, but it's happened, and that means I'll have to tell them everything.

Well, almost everything.

"Put your head between your legs," Rylee says, stroking my back while I do as she says and drag air into my lungs.

When my head clears, I sit up, and try not to stare at Lucy, whose head is swiveling between John, Rylee, and me, her expression stunned.

"Gran, this is Lucy Phillips," Rylee says. "My sister."

Her glare is accusatory, like she knows I've had a hand in keeping them apart all these years.

"Hello, Lucy." I shake her hand, and it's as cold as mine. "How did you two discover your connection?"

"I've been curious about Mom for years, so I sent my DNA to an ancestry website, hoping to find family that may link me to her." Rylee glances at her father and pats the empty chair beside her. "I also wondered if finding someone related to Dad might help discover his true identity." She smiles at Lucy. "Turns out, it has."

John sits next to Rylee, not taking his eyes off Lucy. "I'm sorry. I can't remember anything about you. I have dissociative amnesia."

"That's okay," Lucy says, her smile soft and understanding. "I'm just blown away we get to meet now. I lost Mom recently, so this is surreal."

I know what John's going to ask before he opens his mouth, but I don't stop him. It's too late for secrets now.

"I'm sorry for your loss. Who was your mother?"

"Ava Reynolds. I discovered after she died she was Cora Medville's only child and her father, Spencer Radley, helped her escape Arcania when she was pregnant with me."

I search John's face for a flicker of recognition, but thankfully, there's nothing.

"Ava," he murmurs, a frown appearing between his brow. "I don't remember…"

"That's okay," Lucy and Rylee say in unison, and a lump of emotion lodges in my throat. I can see the two of them becoming close. Where does that leave me?

John looks at me. "You said I worked at Arcania. Was I close with Ava?"

I nod, needing to give him some snippet of the truth. "You loved each other very much. You were making plans to find a place near Arcania and raise your child together. Next thing I know, you arrived here with no memory, and I heard Ava died. I assumed the trauma of her death had caused your amnesia and I didn't want to cause you further pain, so I never told you what I knew."

Confusion clouds his eyes, but before he can ask anything else, Lucy's cell rings.

"Sorry," she says, glancing at the screen. "Whoever it is, I'll call them back."

"Answer it," I say, glad for the distraction.

She gives a brief nod and answers the call. I hear "Yes, I'm Lucy Phillips," swiftly followed by "Oh no," her pallor startling.

"I'll be there as soon as I can," Lucy says, before disconnecting the call. She's visibly trembling and Rylee tentatively touches her arm.

"Is everything okay, Lucy?"

Lucy stares at Rylee blindly and blinks several times before responding. "That was the police. Spencer's body has been found washed up on the beach at Arcania. Looks like a diving accident, faulty equipment..."

She bursts into tears and both Rylee and John rush to comfort her, bracketing her on each side. I can't hear what they're saying, but I'm glad Lucy has someone to comfort her. Losing a grandfather she'd only recently found can't be easy.

While I struggle to hide my relief that Spencer is finally out of our lives.

FIFTY

LEAH

NOW

I'll do whatever it takes to protect my family and now that Spencer is dead, Rylee and John are safe.

Because Spencer could've told them everything.

He could've jogged John's memory.

John could've remembered everything and who knows how he would've reacted to learning Spencer had tried to kill him.

I could tell John that his name is Sam.

That I witnessed Spencer try to drown him.

That I rescued him and brought him back to The Haven.

He didn't walk into The Haven in search of refuge. By the time I got to him after Spencer left him for dead and dragged him into my boat, he'd been unconscious.

And not breathing.

I'd given him CPR, thankful I'd paid attention in a Health class in high school, and revived him. But he'd been unresponsive when his eyes opened, almost catatonic, and by the time we got back to The Haven, I feared the worst. That a lack of oxygen for however long had caused irreversible brain damage.

But once we got to the house, he spoke, though it didn't take long to figure out he couldn't remember what had just happened. In fact, he had no memory at all and when the doctor had confirmed the dissociative amnesia, I'd been relieved.

Sam had always been a nice kid. We'd got along well at Arcania. So if I could nurse him back to health, I'd do it.

But the longer he stayed with me and didn't regain his memory, the more I believed my saving him had been fate's way of delivering me the child I always wanted.

Sam/John became my son, and I didn't want him remembering.

Falling for Robyn put all that at risk.

I knew they had plans to leave me and I couldn't let that happen. What if they chanced across Arcania and John remembered everything? It might've ruined him and I couldn't risk it. He was too precious to me after the few years we'd lived together and bonded.

That woman could've been responsible for me losing my son, so I did the only thing I could.

I got rid of her.

Blackmailing her was the easy part. She left and stayed away.

Until a few months ago, when she asked me to meet her in town. She had the audacity to ask me to deliver a letter to Rylee. That she wanted to reunite with her daughter, get to know her.

As if.

We argued. I tried to grab the letter from her and tear it

up. But as we struggled, I realized there was an easier way to ensure she stayed away.

I asked her to meet me by the wharf at nine that night. I told her Rylee loved going out on the water with me and we did it several times a week. I said they could spend some one-on-one time together in the boat for however long they needed while I waited on the dock.

She believed me.

I knew there'd be no-one around to see us when she boarded my boat and we headed out. I hid my relief as she drank an entire cup of coffee laced with rat poison, meaning she was dead before she hit the water five miles offshore, heavy chains binding her feet and hands so she'd never resurface.

I rejoiced that Robyn could never take Rylee from me as she'd once tried to take John.

I'd done what I had to do to protect those I love.

Spencer is gone too, and I'd do it all again.

Maybe I'm no better than all those who killed at Arcania? Harlan and Cora and Spencer, ever if his attempt at murder failed.

But I've done what I've done out of love.

Can they say the same?

EPILOGUE

JOHN

My heart is full as I watch Rylee and Lucy laugh at Leah's clumsy attempt to slide a sponge cake out of a silicone pan. Leah knows a strawberry jelly filled cake covered in whipped cream is Lucy's favorite and it's nice to see her making an effort with my eldest.

I still can't believe I have another daughter. It's like being bestowed a precious gift after having the memory of her mother wiped. I can't remember Ava despite trying. I've spent countless hours talking with Lucy, having her recount details of her mother, poring over photos together, but nothing.

It's fine, because I have all the family I need now.

Rylee is dividing her time between The Haven and Manhattan. Lucy has been showing her around New York City and I'm glad. Rylee needs to spread her wings. I know she's been reluctant to leave because of me, but now we have answers to so many questions, she's okay.

She told me everything about Robyn: why she left me, the letters, Leah's blackmail, Freda's involvement. I hired a PI to find Robyn, but nothing has turned up. Robyn vanished after she last visited Edgewater Bay and there's nothing more to be done.

Because if I probe further, I'm afraid of what I might find.

Of what Leah may have done to Robyn.

I've read Robyn's letters, so I know about the charm bracelet. It sounds exactly like the bracelet I found washed up on the beach in town four weeks ago. From its tarnish, it had been in the water for months, and I can only surmise how Leah disposed of Robyn.

I've seen firsthand what Leah is capable of in the name of protecting me.

I saw her tamper with Spencer's diving gear that day at Arcania when she tried her utmost to prevent me from meeting him.

I know why she did it: she didn't want me remembering him and what he did to me.

But what Leah doesn't know is that it was too late.

I remembered everything the moment I laid eyes on Arcania.

The memory of Spencer taking me to the cove, of saying he'd teach me to swim, of his hands on my shoulders shoving me underwater and holding me down, of the terrifying sensation of water filling my mouth until...nothing.

Spencer tried to kill me, and the second I remembered, I knew I couldn't have him anywhere near my daughter. Rylee was so enthused about working at Arcania it would've been hard to stop her, so I did what any loving father would do.

Removed the threat.

Leah had barely made a dent in tampering with Spencer's diving equipment, so I finished the job. While Spencer knew I couldn't swim, he didn't count on me paying attention when he gave diving lessons to Arcania's employees. Who would've thought, that information I thought I'd never need because I had no intention of going near the water would ultimately save my family?

I remembered the important details: checking fins and tanks, breathing through primary and alternative respirators, ensuring depth gauges worked correctly.

Because if those depth gauges don't work, a diver can misjudge how much air is in his tank. If that air runs out too soon and you're too deep, you panic and rise to the surface too fast, resulting in decompression sickness and potentially death.

I'd fiddled with Spencer's depth gauge, ensuring he wouldn't have time to do the usual decompression stop as he rose to the surface. His panic at not being able to breathe would mean nitrogen bubbles became trapped in his bloodstream and a bad case of the bends resulted in his death.

Spencer's experience with diving meant he rarely checked his gear. He'd been doing it for forty years and I'd witnessed him give nothing more than a cursory glance at his tanks and gauges because he was too cocky, too over-confident.

I counted on it. And ultimately, it led to his demise.

Of course the police ruled his death an accident. A faulty depth gauge has resulted in other divers dying. I knew I would get away with it.

Am I sorry for what I did? No. Because like Leah, I'll do anything to protect the ones I love.

I made sure Spencer Hadley could never harm anyone in my family again. And to think, Lucy would've always been a link between us, her grandfather and her father...

That man robbed me of twenty-four years of my daughter's life and I'll never forgive him for that.

He deserved to die.

And I don't feel a flicker of remorse.

I hope you enjoyed The Haven.
Please consider leaving a review.
And check out BANISH.

★★★★★ **THE VAMPIRE DIARIES L.J. Smith, #1 New York Times bestselling author, says** *"Nicola Marsh has done a masterful job at creating a supernatural thriller full of unexpected twists and turns...Absolutely love the book, ten out of ten."*

I HAVE *one week to annihilate my enemy and save my soul.*

After my ex-boyfriend dies and my mom's alcoholism sparks another psychotic episode, I flee my small hometown of Broadwater and head to New York City to stay with my bohemian aunt—a Wicca High Priestess.

I revel in the anonymity of a big city. I make good friends and meet a new guy, sexy geek Ronan, a saxophonist who prefers jazz to pop.

But my newfound peace is obliterated when I glimpse a dead body in one of Ronan's music clips—and I'm the only one who can see it. Worse, I recognize the body...murdered a week into the future.

I don't believe in the supernatural, despite my family's Wicca background. But as secrets start to unravel, evil is closer than I think and I'm powerless to stop the inevitable...

READ BANISH NOW!

Have you read the first book in this duo, THE RETREAT?

You CAN STAY, *but you may never leave...*

FOR GUESTS who spend a week at Arcania, a wellness retreat in the Outer Banks for those wanting to digitally detox, the gothic mansion is a welcome haven. Others aren't so lucky.

When Lucy's mother dies unexpectedly and a mysterious Viking tattoo reveals a link to Arcania, Lucy books a week at the retreat. Cora Medville, the owner, seems welcoming enough, but soon the creepy house and its inhabitants are urging Lucy to flee, or risk dying like some before her.

Four decades earlier, runaway Cora is smitten by Arcania and the dashing owner Harlan. Craving a sense of belonging, she finds it with her new family and their majestic mansion.

But when residents start disappearing and she learns the terrifying truth, who can she trust?

How far will she go to protect Arcania's sordid secrets?

Read THE RETREAT now!

.

ACKNOWLEDGMENTS

If you've read the first book in this duo, The Retreat, you'll know how much I loved getting swept away to haunting mansions and their secretive inhabitants in my teens through devouring books by Victoria Holt and Daphne du Maurier.

Those stories fuelled my love of all things gothic so imagine my surprise four decades later when these stories, The Retreat and The Haven, marched into my imagination, demanding to be told.

I hope you have as much fun reading them as I did creating them.

As always, bringing a book to fruition isn't a solo gig, so with thanks to the following:

MaryAnn Schaefer for her proofreading skills, and helping me with my Aussie-isms!

Debbie at The Cover Collection, for creating yet another fab cover that encapsulates the vibe of the story so perfectly.

Erica, the manager at Robinsons Books at The Glen, your support and enthusiasm for my books is much appreciated.

The members of Nicola Marsh's Readers Room on Facebook, our book chats are always fun.

Soraya and Natalie, my author buddies, always there for me.

Martin, you'll be pleased no husbands are killed off in this one, LOL!

My folks, for their never-ending support.

My gorgeous boys, love you so much.

The readers who signed up to read ARCs, thanks for taking the time to read and review.

And last but not least, to all the BookTokers, bookstagrammers, readers, bloggers, booksellers, librarians, and everyone in the bookish world who read, promote, and sell my books. I appreciate you so much!

FREE BOOK AND MORE

SIGN UP TO NICOLA'S NEWSLETTER for a free book!

Read Nicola's newest feel-good romance **DID NOT FINISH**

Or her gothic **THE RETREAT**

Try the **CARTWRIGHT BROTHERS** duo

FASCINATION

PERFECTION

The **WORKPLACE LIAISONS** duo

THE BOSS

THE CEO

Try the **BASHFUL BRIDES** series

NOT THE MARRYING KIND

NOT THE ROMANTIC KIND

NOT THE DARING KIND

NOT THE DATING KIND

The **CREATIVE IN LOVE** series

THE GRUMPY GUY

THE SHY GUY

THE GOOD GUY

Try the **BOMBSHELLS** series

BEFORE (FREE!)

BRASH

BLUSH

BOLD

BAD

BOMBSHELLS BOXED SET

The **WORLD APART** series

WALKING THE LINE (FREE!)

CROSSING THE LINE

TOWING THE LINE

BLURRING THE LINE

WORLD APART BOXED SET

The **HOT ISLAND NIGHTS** duo

WICKED NIGHTS

WANTON NIGHTS

The **BOLLYWOOD BILLIONAIRES** series

FAKING IT

MAKING IT

The **LOOKING FOR LOVE** series

LUCKY LOVE

CRAZY LOVE

SAPPHIRES ARE A GUY'S BEST FRIEND

THE SECOND CHANCE GUY

Check out Nicola's website for a full list of her books.

And read her other romances as Nikki North.

'MILLIONAIRE IN THE CITY' series.

LUCKY

COCKY

CRAZY

FANCY

FLIRTY

FOLLY

MADLY

Check out the **ESCAPE WITH ME** series.

DATE ME

LOVE ME

DARE ME

TRUST ME

FORGIVE ME

Try the **LAW BREAKER** series

THE DEAL MAKER

THE CONTRACT BREAKER

About the Author

USA TODAY bestselling and multi-award winning author Nicola Marsh writes page-turning fiction to keep you up all night.

She's published 80 books and sold 8 million copies worldwide.

She currently writes contemporary romance and domestic suspense.

She's also a Waldenbooks, Bookscan, Amazon, iBooks and Barnes & Noble bestseller, a RBY (Romantic Book of the Year) and National Readers' Choice Award winner, and a multi-finalist for a number of awards including the Romantic Times Reviewers' Choice Award, HOLT Medallion, Booksellers' Best, Golden Quill, Laurel Wreath, and More than Magic.

A physiotherapist for thirteen years, she now adores writing full time, raising her two dashing young heroes, sharing fine food with family and friends, and her favorite, curling up with a good book!